To Master the Tides

Josephine Borgia

Published by Josephine Borgia, 2022.

This is a work of fiction. Similarities to real people, places, or events are entirely coincidental.

TO MASTER THE TIDES

First edition. June 20, 2022.

Copyright © 2022 Josephine Borgia.

ISBN: 979-8201887391

Written by Josephine Borgia.

One

Frederick Estibus sat up on the edge of the bed and lit a cigarette. Lady Fitton didn't care for the smell, but he did it anyway. She tsked but said nothing else. Frederick inhaled deeply and stared at the cigarette, mired in thought. Would he go through with it? Ought he to go through with it? She would have his throat but there was nothing for it. Cuthbert had said he must. There was no arguing with Cuthbert. He took his last drag of the smoke and squandered the half of it in the tray. Margery sighed and rolled over to run a hand across Frederick's broad shoulders.

"I'll need to be finished with you after this, Margery," he said, without turning around. The hand on his back jerked away. She gave him a little slap on the shoulder and laughed.

"You oughtn't to talk that way unless you mean it," she said. "What have I done now? You should say it outright."

Frederick turned now and gazed a long time at her. She lay back on the pillow, hand behind her head to preserve her chignon. She insisted her hair stay neat even during the most violent of their love-making. In the end, she was always on top. She clutched the covers up to her chest but allowed her thigh to peek out. Fredrick thought she fancied it an alluring position, but her veins stood out dark blue against her colorless skin. At first, Frederick had thought her like marble, like the masterpieces he had seen on his grand tour. Now she looked dull and weathered to him, like a forsaken gargoyle on a mausoleum.

"Come back to bed," she said, holding out a hand strained towards him. A tinge of desperation creased around her eyes, but she wasn't afraid. Frederick could see that. He ignored her hand and crossed the room to her writing desk. The fire burned hot, and he did not bother with his clothes. "What are you doing?" Margery asked as he rummaged through the desk. "I can't tell you how silly you look."

"The letters," said Frederick.

"Do you want to read them?" They did that in the beginning; reading each other's letters out loud, overacting as ridiculously as possible. Things were amusing then; they could laugh at themselves.

"No," he said. He grabbed them up in great handfuls. There were many accumulated over their nine-year affair. He paused over a few of them, recognizing his immature hand of 17. She had captured him when he was a child. She was young to look at then as well. It was not as if she were his only. It was understood that he could do as he liked so long as he came back to her. He walked to the fire and threw the lot on the blaze.

"What are you doing?!" she said, her voice rising to a shriek. She crawled to the edge of the bed, still clutching the bed coverings to her chest.

"I can't have evidence," said Frederick. "Cuthbert says I must marry."

"Oh, your brother!" Lady Fitton said with some relief. She dropped the sheet and walked to her toilet table, taking her time to put on her dressing gown. "Is that all? We will need to pause some weeks, I expect, until your new wife is tired of you. You'll see that's how it goes."

Frederick frowned. He had come to her that evening with the idea of ending things straight off, but it had come to this in her room instead. The scent of her always made him react that certain way and now they were here. She prattled on, sitting at her gaudy table, in her gaudy ruffled dressing gown, saying gaudy things about when they ought to renew their affair—in the spring, of course. Lord Fitton, her husband, always went to the continent in the spring.

Frederick intended to end it right as soon as he had arrived. He really had but she swept him up in the whole of the moment and then there they were again. Naked in the room which he told himself once was ornate and wonderful in the classic style. Now it was only gaudy, as was she. He felt a pang at that thought. He ought not to be cruel.

"I really must be finished with you, entirely, you understand? Cuthbert says..."

"Enough of him!" Lady Fitton stamped her foot a little. "I know he seems the paragon of propriety to you but he's not so polite as you think. You hear things of people if you listen in the right places." She walked over to Frederick and laid a hand on his cheek. "And now you should listen to me." Her smile was sweet, but her eyes were not. Frederick took a step back and clenched his fists. He looked away from her and at the embers of the letters curling in the overbuilt fire. He was still naked, and the shadows cast by the flickering light accentuated the curves of his muscular frame and the stubborn line of his jaw.

JOSEPHINE BORGIA

"My mind is made up," Frederick said. "I am to marry, in a few months I'm told, and we are well shut." He felt like a toddler stamping his foot.

Lady Fitton took a step back. Color trickled up from her neckline until red engulfed her entire face. She contained herself but fell to her knees, clutching his thighs and burying her face in his leg. He felt moisture against his thigh. *Ah! She's got up some tears.* He was glad of it. He never knew her to shed any true emotion and that solidified his resolve rather than cracking it. She must have sensed something of the sort. She ceased her crying and turned her head, moving her lips to take him in her mouth. Frederick wasn't up to it, so soon after they lay together, but a grunt escaped his lips. She put more effort into the work, but Frederick withdrew himself with the utmost care. Still on her knees, Lady Fitton pleaded with him.

"You can't!"

Frederick said nothing and sidestepped her to reach for his clothes on the floor. She anticipated him, however, and dove for them. "You cannot have these until you take it back! You won't? Lady Fitton cast his clothes on the fire on top of the letters. "Well, then!"

"Margery!"

"Don't call me that!" She flew at him in a violent rage. "You have no right be so familiar ever again!" Frederick chose to protect his manhood. He shut his eyes tight while she clawed his face and screamed obscenities. "We'll see how the new little bitch likes your face with the marks of your mistress on it! I'd throw your manhood on the fire too if I could! Get out! Get out of my house! I'll send my husband after you with pistols!"

TO MASTER THE TIDES

"I can't leave like this," Frederick pointed out and requested some clothes between strikes. Most missed their mark in her fit but a few nails drug trenches across his cheek. He was reduced to cowering in a ball on the floor to protect both his manhood and his eyes. Lady Fitton's energy finally wore down and she let off hitting him. She pulled on a dressing robe. He tried to speak to her again, to ask for some clothing so he could leave. She answered him by pulling hard on the bell over and over again. Many servants came to the door and banged on it, asking if she had come to harm. Lady Fitton swung the French doors open wide and pointed at Frederick on the floor.

"Get him out! As you see him! I want him out the front door and I do not care what becomes of him!" She ignored the servants' protests and slammed the doors shut.

The servants took Frederick up by the arms and marched him to the front of the house. They tossed him out the door, face down in the snow. There he lay, hoping he would die where he was.

Frederick lifted his head off the ground a moment to look around him. The snow was light but had stopped only that afternoon. Lady Fitton's carriage brought him there as always, but he had been looking forward to the walk home. The sky cleared and the moon was bright. He liked the muffled quiet of a snow-covered world. There was a singular aloneness about it, one that couldn't be gotten any other way. Now it was all pain. Even if he were clothed this minute, his feet hurt all at once from the cold.

He knew not how long he lay on the ground before a faint whinny sounded up the drive. A small carriage clattered behind. Whether delirious from the cold or were the clacking of hooves were muffled by the snow, he could not tell. He eased up on his elbow and squinted up into the dark. Through the haze of near-unconsciousness, Frederick saw a man rein in the horse and hop out of the trailing phaeton. The silhouette of the round man with the babyish puffy cheeks loomed over Frederick. He knew that form well enough: his brother, Cuthbert, had come for him.

"I'm proud of you," Cuthbert said. "I didn't think you'd do it."

Eying his brother, Frederick's teeth clenched too hard to even chatter. Cuthbert hauled him up by the armpits, stumbling into the snow himself. "Come," he said. "We'll share the cart cloak as we did when we were boys."

Fredrick climbed onto the phaeton's seat next to his brother. He wrapped his half of the cloak around himself as they set off. He had to hunch his hulking frame to share properly and keep the wind out of the gap in the front. He was unnaturally tall and what Cuthbert had in width, Frederick made up in height. The snow in his curly hair melted in his hair, which stuck lank and irritating to his forehead. He pulled the blanket over his head so his hair wouldn't freeze there. It was such a cold night, and the frost was even steaming out of Cuthbert's mutton chops.

"Have you a smoke rolled?" asked Frederick when his teeth had finally stopped chattering. Cuthbert handed him his case. Frederick shared his mild gratitude for the cigarette and the ride and told his brother as much.

"No trouble, no trouble," said Cuthbert, puffing out his chest. "I knew you had to fuck her before you left, so I bode my time. Don't look so offended man. Do you deny it, the state I found you in? It's a pity you couldn't make a clean break of it but there it is."

"It doesn't signify what I did," said Frederick, hunching down still further. "It's finished with her." He stiffened when he said that. The realization of it spread through his stomach like blood seeping into one's clothes after a deep cut. It had hit him just now. "It's finished with her," he repeated, more emphatically.

Lady Fitton's reaction was nothing. She would always let you know, rather forcefully, if she didn't care for what you said. She likely didn't believe him. Throwing him naked in the snow was nothing—nothing at all. He thought of what would happen when she finally knew he wasn't coming to her anymore. He took another long drag on his cigarette until he coughed.

"Of course, it isn't finished," said Cuthbert, laughing at his brother's fit. "It never is with that type of woman. I'm sore vexed you were caught up with her in the first place, but you were young when it happened and none of us knew you'd amount to anything. Thought you ought to have a patron, at least, but you know all that. I mean for you to come to the city with me, day after next. We'll let her stew a bit, find a new toy. If she can fancy she left you, so much the better."

She wouldn't find a new toy. Frederick knew that. It was more than a pastime to her, as it was to Cuthbert, but Cuthy could only judge things as he saw them for himself.

Frederick was glad to be shuffled off to the townhouse. There, he would meet Isabella Fortridge—the one Cuthbert had chosen for him. She was a cousin of some sort of Cuthbert's wife. Frederick hoped there was no family resemblance. Mrs. Lucy Estibus was a good sort and pretty before the many children. Now, as Cuthbert described her, she was like the well-kept women of the Renaissance masterpieces.

Isabella's papa was interested in the fortune Frederick inherited from an uncle with no heir. Cuthbert had been passed over as he was to receive their father's country seat ... someday. So now the second son was rich and the elder was anxious to cultivate it. Propriety and connections were of the utmost importance, but Frederick maddeningly didn't seem to care about these things. Even so, Frederick was glad to see the house as they pulled up the drive. They both still lived there. Cuthbert laid in wait like a vulture, and Frederick simply existed.

The snow fell again, in earnest this time. Frederick wondered if Cuthbert was still thinking of driving into town tomorrow. They could very well be snowed in for the rest of the season, even with the family barouche and four. The phaeton came to a halt in the drive in front of the great house, and a servant came out to take the reins. Cuthbert was still talking on, but Frederick had ceased to listen. "Make sure the horse gets an extra treat tonight," he said to the servant who took the reins. Frederick pulled the carriage blanket tight to keep out the draft and eased his way out of the carriage. Despite Frederick's protests of needing to put on clothes, Cuthbert succeeded in corralling him into the sitting room for a nightcap.

"Nonsense," Cuthbert said, waving away the difficulty. "That's what servants are for. They'll bring you a robe. I'll have them stoke up a good fire and we'll get some whiskey in your gut. That ought to warm you."

TO MASTER THE TIDES

Soon Frederick was installed in a wingback chair, feet on an ottoman as close as he dared to the fire. He had donned a nightshirt but refused to give up the carriage blanket. Frederick sat across from him and was already refilling his glass. His puffy cheeks grew red from the drink as much as from the fire. Frederick could tell his brother wanted to make a night of it. There was no getting around it. While he didn't mind the drink, especially now that the warmth crept through his stomach in that steely way, he would have much rather been quiet. Frederick loved his brother, but Cuthbert had a way of wearing all the energy from him. It left him sapped while Cuthbert only seemed more wound and ready for action. Frederick would let him ramble and hope the drink took effect early. He would go to bed once his brother was snoring in his chair.

"When do you take possession of Danforth?" Cuthbert asked. Frederick was glad he chose not to rehash recent events.

"In the spring," said Frederick. "I shall go up as soon as the roads are good."

"Ah, perfect. I expect you'll wish to marry before summer."

"If she'll have me."

"Nonsense, nonsense. It's all arranged, all arranged. She's a lovely thing, too. You will both look splendid next to one another. You'll thank me once you see her. And such a lovely smile."

Frederick raised an eyebrow at his brother. "You think so much of her? Why didn't you marry her?"

"Me?! Oh, more nonsense from you. She was too young, then, when I was to marry. Only 15, you see."

JOSEPHINE BORGIA

"So, you would have, if she'd been older?" said Frederick, already feeling the first effects of the whiskey on an empty stomach. He gave his brother a wry smile. "I can't have you chasing my future wife, can I?"

"You are a fiend and no doubt!" Cuthbert finished off his second glass turning still redder and pouring another. "I can't think of anyone who wouldn't marry her. I was only speaking of impossibilities, not my own designs. You are a fool, Frederick."

"Perhaps I am," said Frederick. "But not for teasing you." He leaned back in his chair and stared into the fire.

"You, with that melancholy of yours," said Cuthbert, leaping at the chance to draw the conversation away from himself. "You need to snap out of it. I said things are all arranged but she won't want to care for you if you're always moping about. No one cares for people like that. They let them be and then all of a sudden, you're 'being' by yourself. Do what I do. Take a brisk walk or have some spirits. Spirits for your spirit. That's the thing. Had you ever tried being happy? You used to be so when we were young. You'd take pleasure in the trees, for Christ's sake. Maybe you expended it all then and you've none left. But you'll need to snap out of it before we meet Miss Fortridge. Isabella Fortridge is your betrothed. Can you remember that? You are so bad with names sometimes. But you must remember to be jolly. We're going to a party, after all. I know how foolish these people can be, but you ought to at least try more. Here, have some more whiskey."

"You can't expect me to be jolly just now, can you?" asked Frederick, holding out his glass, though it wasn't empty. "I've had a rough night of it."

TO MASTER THE TIDES

"Serves you right," said Cuthbert, pouring more whiskey into the glass spilling only a little. As tipsy as he was, wasting alcohol was a capital offense. "If you want to get rid of them, you have to stop fucking them."

"You know this from experience?"

"Well, not my own, if that's what you mean! But many of my colleagues at Cambridge, yes: many of them, a rowdy bunch. Many of them had a woman here and there that could not be got rid of all because they kept them dangling. And what did they expect? They didn't stop with their pleasure and of course, the women got with child eventually. It always happens eventually, and then they were stuck. In your case it was different. She was so old. It wasn't likely but still. She is one you ought not to lead on. I can only hope when she sees your new wife, she will reconcile herself to the facts."

"Perhaps we ought to stay in town at first," said Frederick. The horror of the women crossing paths had not occurred to him. "We could avoid this set altogether until Margery has gotten used to the idea."

"No, no," said Cuthbert. "You had better commit all at once. She'll soon see. We'll spend some time in town and she will have found someone else. That is how it will be. You'll see. You'll see."

Two

Frederick was not surprised, and a bit relieved when he was told the trip into town was delayed—. Cuthbert didn't bother to tell him in person only sending a short note. Cuthbert was going out somehow. Frederick felt a twinge of pity for whatever horse his brother had chosen to take. He jammed his toast and went to the window, nibbling a bit at the crust. He had no appetite this morning but supposed he ought to eat.

The fields were a blinding blanket of show that extended far beyond the house. The gamekeeper's cottage that sat just on the border between Danforth and his father's estate was a dot off in the distance with a trickle of smoke coming from it. The keeper must be fair buried. He was a crusty sort, though, well-hardened by the elements, and was likely prepared. The great house itself was on the other side of the property and well unreachable in weather such as this; really, any spit of weather as the road to it was so bad. Frederick's uncle had died a bachelor and preferred to be left alone. The old man had always rather liked Frederick and it was from him that Frederick had gotten his taste for philosophy.

A book of the stuff still lay on Frederick's chair by his hearth. The servants had stoked up a good fire for him and he settled in to read. It was some stoic or other and the words seemed to jumble up. His thoughts trailed off as they do when he was in one of his moods. Before long he was staring into the flames thinking those thoughts again. The ones that took him out of himself and made him fancy he was dancing with the wisps of fire in the grate.

I wonder, he thought. *Why was I born to this and not that? The gamekeeper's lot. I'm sure I could keep game just as well as any. And why am I looking out from these eyes, just now, in just this year? Has anyone ever really realized they will never really look at their own face? A reflection is an imperfect thing. I know I have a mole just under my left cheekbone, but I can never really examine it. What if I'd been born first, just as I am, but first? Would I be out in the snow just now? Or would I be sitting here with Socrates and all these thoughts? What if I hadn't been born at all? Or died here now, just as I am? How would they all react?*

Frederick frowned. Those thoughts always left an emptiness in his chest. They made him hungry for more, always more knowledge but the knowledge he wanted wasn't there to be had. Why, why, why? Because God willed it so. Frederick found it difficult to believe that God cared that much for him and easier to think that he was a side effect of an encounter between his parents. It was also very unlikely that anyone cared much for him.

Perhaps Margery did. For her, he was there to do with as she pleased. There was a certain thrill in that when he first came to her. A thrill in doing what wasn't supposed to be done. She was 29 then and still in good looks. He was a boy, though he fancied himself very grown, going about an adult intrigue with a peer's wife. He had gotten a high from it, one that he could never control. Anything could be sacrificed for it and then, as he was no one, no one cared what he did. Lord Fitton was away most of the time and too stupid to notice. Margery wasn't stupid. She read a great deal and listened to Frederick in the beginning when he first came home from the university, parroting back all he had learned.

"It's all well and good that you know Socrates says that and Plato says this," she'd said, rapping him with her fan, "but which one do you think is true?"

"Well, aren't they both?" said a bewildered 18-year-old Frederick.

"Of course not!" said Margery, rolling her eyes. "If you understood them rather than just memorize, you'd see that you just spouted off two contradictory ideas. Ponder it a bit. I want to know what you think."

His uncle had taught him to love thought but Margery taught him to find his own.

There was less and less of that, however, as the years went by, replaced by more sweat and urgency. Being Lady Fitton had worn her down and she clung to Frederick as if he were the incarnation of her youth. His thrill was gone, too, and he went through the motions simply because that was what his body did with her. She became spiteful and vengeful as well, so he no longer took pleasure in allowing her to be his master. A mild spark of panic interrupted his thoughts. Perhaps he ought to send her a note today. He threw his book on the floor. No. Cuthbert had been right. He didn't care for that, either.

Wind rattled the windows and he stoked up the fire. By the light outside, he fancied he slept most of the day away. It wasn't too early. He hobbled to the bell on his still-tender feet and rang for some wine.

TO MASTER THE TIDES

As it turned out, they did not make their way to town until well into the springtime, after Frederick had taken over Danforth.

The first night in town, Lord Estibus was to give a small party. The dinner itself was a tiresome affair, as it always was at the Estibus townhome. The dining room was stuffy, dimly lit, and Gothic. Lord Estibus had no intention of updating the dark room, either. It had a feel that someone had been murdered there. Not recently, mind you, but perhaps many people, long ago during one of the many exchanges of power among the royal families. The room conjured images of young princesses stripped of their jewels yet still crying because they hadn't gotten cake.

Frederick was not seated near Isabella at dinner. She was far down the long table animatedly chatting with Cuthbert, who took up his dead mother's seat at the foot. Frederick was near the head with his father on one side and Mrs. Whetherton on the other. She was mean-spirited and frightfully stupid. She had quite a large nose, but her hair remained raven black even well into her 40s. She had just married her second husband and would be moving to their county home after the season in town. Frederick was sorry for it and sorry for Mr. Whetherton. He was a good-natured fellow and inexplicably seemed to adore her. He would realize soon enough. She was currently going on about the abysmal quality of servants at their townhome and hoped the country folk weren't "incomp-tant," as she pronounced it—and she pronounced it thus fairly often. Frederick would cringe each time she said it and cast a subvert dirty look at Cuthbert's wife, who had done the arrangement.

JOSEPHINE BORGIA

It was a small crowd for dinner that night. Many weren't in town yet. The roads were passable but still not good. Still, Cuthbert seemed in a frenzy to get his brother wed and somehow persuaded the guests to brave the mud.

There were the Fortridges: Isabella and her mother and father; the Whethertons. There were two lawyers, Kilkenny and Falcom, Lord Estibus knew from his club. They were an odd pair to be seen together: Kilkenny was a ginger Irishman, but not a bad chap for all that. Falcom was old and stiff and looked like he wished the Puritans from the old days were still in charge. Their wives seemed to be the best of friends so perhaps that was the cause of it. Cuthbert and his wife took up two more spots, and two seats remained vacant.

Lord Estibus hadn't said who was supposed to take the empty chairs and Frederick didn't care. Cuthbert was the sycophant when it came to his father's circle. Frederick intended to settle in the country and cared little for invitations.

He glanced thoughtfully at Isabella. She was pretty and very young. *Perhaps she might not care for the isolation.* He stopped chewing for a moment. Was this really happening? Of course. Everything his father or his brother determined should happen to him, did. All but the money from his uncle. His uncle had done that to spite them. Lord Estibus had tried to persuade the uncle to leave it to Cuthbert. Then Cuthbert might have the consequence needed to bring the proper esteem back to their declining name and peerage. Instead, it had gone to Frederick.

Frederick dreaded the drawing room after dinner and the obligatory small talk. Drinking brandy and smoking with the men only required his presence. He could puff and grunt and not say a thing or offer an idea; otherwise, he was free to think what he liked and disdain whom he pleased, letting the others bluster. In mixed company, even the men talked of nothing, thinking they were pleasing the women, while the women prattled about trifles, thinking they were pleasing the men. He would have to speak with Isabella. That was certain. Perhaps if he could draw her into a real conversation there might be hope. The real conversations wore him the most, however, he would take that exhaustion over the other.

A cloud of cigar smoke preceded the men into the drawing room, as twisted and dark as the dining. Frederick fancied himself emerging from hell and the smoke that of brimstone. He tried to remain in the back of the crowd, but Cuthbert pulled him forward. On the sofa in front of the fire was Isabella and Mrs. Whetherton and it was to this that Cuthbert dragged Frederick. Cuthbert and Frederick stood stupidly next to the women, drawing breath every so often to attempt to announce their presence, but Mrs. Whetherton's endless stream of words would not cease.

Frederick took a good long look at Isabella. She listened most earnestly and politely to the other lady's ravings. Her cheeks flushed a delicate pink for being too close to the fire. Her hair shone chestnut even in that dim light and the bits that escaped her twists, curled thick around her neck. He thought unaccountably of his mother. The skin was the same, the teasing smile she cast them when she glanced their way, the way she spoke to Mrs. Whetherton earnestly as she went on about her troubles at the dressmaker's that day.

"My goodness!" Isabella exclaimed. "It must have been quite an ordeal!" She was enthusiastic in her sympathy yet found the woman foolish. But Isabella was not mocking her interlocutor; instead, she found her endearing.

Frederick took all this in in a moment, though such developed thoughts never spelled themselves out in his head. *She is kind*, was all he thought with somewhat of a shock. He never imagined his father or brother would find him anyone of that sort. He always surmised they would pick someone with what they imagined was his state of melancholy. They were odd beings. His father preferred to live in a murder house yet surround himself with livelihood. They presumed they understood his mood and tried to accommodate it but we're always far off the mark.

It was Isabella who finally dared to interrupt Mrs. Whetherton's tirade.

"I do apologize, Julia, my dear," she said, laying a gentle hand on the lady's arm, "but I do believe these two would like to speak with us."

"Oh, oh, oh!" said Mrs. Whetherton, fanning herself furiously with her lacy hankie. "I'm sure it's you they want to speak to. I'll leave you be. This fire has me overheated and I'm worked up already." She turned to Frederick. "Now, you take good care of my little friend here. If I hear you've been making her sad, I shall never let you forget it!" She gave an obvious wink to Isabella, who nodded in good grace and blamed the fire for her reddened cheeks. Cuthbert bumbled and apologized—to Isabella, not a word to Frederick—making the situation worse until Isabella interrupted.

"Oh, pay that no mind. I am easy on it, I assure you," she said, maintaining the pleasant cadence in her voice. "Is this your brother lurking behind you? With your behavior just now, I don't blame him for hiding."

"Yes, yes," said Cuthbert, even more flustered. "This is Frederick."

Isabella held out her hand and Frederick took it, squeezing a little harder than he might. In truth, he envied her a bit already. She had the ease in the presence of his foolish brother that he had yet to master. She had the right words while he had none. He had none now. Her eyes held questions when she tugged to withdraw her hand, but she smiled wide at him.

"Come, sit with me by the fire," she said. "It's over warm but I confess I catch a chill easily and am not ready to move. I'm sorry I was unable to speak with you before dinner."

Frederick took his seat and leaned back so that he could look at her while they talked but just as easily look away. He asked her about her trip to town. That was an easy thing to ask, and he hoped she would have a lot to say on it. He could "hem" and "is that so?" all he wanted. She did rattle on as animatedly as at dinner. It was pleasant and he could see how it would make her a favorite, but he felt he ought to keep up his end of it and it wore on him. Still, he pulled her on.

"And you say you were stuck around Horley?" he asked? "I do hear it's dreadful there."

"Oh yes," she said. "We all had to get out a push. There was nothing for it. We were all so very muddy and cold the rest of the trip. We stopped in Sidlow to buy new things for the servants. I couldn't let them sit in the cold and be wet the whole way while we were warm in the carriage. Enough of that chilly ride. What about you?"

JOSEPHINE BORGIA

"We didn't get stuck," said Frederick. "I'd say our poor horses had a time of it."

They had. Their hooves were fair-caked by the time they arrived, and Frederick had spent the good part of the evening cleaning them up along with the stablemen. He missed tea on their arrival and endured a talking-to from Cuthbert. His father, oblivious to most things hadn't noticed. He did not tell Isabella all this, though he mulled it over in the uncomfortable silence.

"I hope I get a chance to see your father's library before we leave town," said Isabella, venturing to keep the conversation up. Frederick perked up at that. *Ah, you like books! We may have something to talk about, after all.*

"Would you like to see it now?" asked Frederick.

"Would you show me?"

They walked down the long corridor to the library, taking only a candle. Frederick tried to get a glimpse of her in the light while she stared straight forward. The silence was comfortable to him but her little twittering footsteps next to him disrupted it. The dark suited him. The quiet was a balm on his excitable nerve he always had at parties. She was in his envelope but looking entirely out of place.

She was dressed in dark green that brought out the green in her eyes. Her cheeks pink and her smile as bright as the sun; she was a spring glade to Frederick's deep woods. He was brown, eyes, hair, face always dark and sour. The lines Margery cut in his face were not prominent, but gave him the look of a withered old tree. Isabella could barge in his world, however, and maybe bring it the light of day. If that is what the tide brought to him, perhaps he would take it.

TO MASTER THE TIDES

They pushed through the double doors of the library and Frederick lit a few gas lamps. There was a fire in the hearth and the servant who tended it snored peacefully on the sofa in front. Isabella giggled at him and he spluttered away, apologizing profusely. Frederick excused him and Isabella took the candle to examine titles.

"My father keeps all the newest titles in town, I'm afraid," Frederick said. "All the classics get shipped off to his country home."

"That's sensible of him," said Isabella, picking a book and going to the sofa to examine it. "City guests want to be entertained. I can't read that old stuff."

"What book did you choose?"

"'The Prisoner of Zenda'! I've been dying to read it. I'm surprised your father has it."

"That?" Frederick thought he did well hiding the disappointment in his voice. "That's likely Cuthbert's choice. I'm sure no one will mind if you wish to borrow it."

Isabella clasped the book to her chest and thanked Frederick profusely.

"Oughtn't we get back to the party?" she asked. They went, while, Isabella, encouraged by the gift of the book, prattled on.

"Do you have many horses at Danforth?" she asked.

"Yes, my uncle bred them," Frederick said. "I intend to take up the business. They are wonderful creatures. They understand men better than most men, I think. Gentle, if you treat them right, and loyal."

"I understand your uncle had quite a good reputation as a breeder."

"Very much so, and he taught me a lot."

JOSEPHINE BORGIA

By this time, they were returning to the drawing room, Frederick talking as enthusiastically as Isabella could. He didn't dare look around, as they took seats, but he could feel the stares of his father and brother, smugly looking on as well as the others in the room.

The two of them were on show tonight and he knew his family was congratulating itself on a well-made match. He wondered what she felt underneath the small talk and he wished he had taken the time to ask her when they were alone. Still, she let him go on in a way he never was allowed with anyone else. Her smiles and encouragement were more than enough to keep him talking and it passed through his mind that this might not be an unpleasant way to spend his life. They could share books, he supposed, and if she could read one of his, he ought to give hers a try.

"There are our tardy guests!" said Lord Estibus, interrupting everyone's dialogue. Frederick shivered as the doors to the drawing room opened and let in a brief gust. He turned to see the two who had missed dinner.

"Lord and Lady Fitton!" announced the servant.

Three

Frederick turned immediately. Isabella noticed the sudden pallor in his face but said nothing. She glanced at the newcomers then down at her book, squeezing it tight in her hand.

"I'm going to put this with my things, so I don't lose it," she said, getting up.

Frederick was happy to be left alone to stew. He crossed his arms and sunk into the sofa, hoping to become invisible. He should get up, he knew, but he wouldn't. He inhaled deeply to calm himself. The wood from the fire was pungent and soothing but a familiar too-sweet smell reached his nostrils. Jasmine and thyme. Lady Fitton's sachet. The smell was stronger now. She was coming. He stared fixedly at the fire, stuffing down the mixed emotions of dread and arousal her scent evoked. What ought he to say to her? *I'm no longer accountable to her,* he kept reminding himself.

The jasmine was stronger than ever, and he felt a gentle touch on his shoulder. He turned to see Margery, looking down on him. The look on her face was inscrutable. Was it hatred or sorrow? Her eyes were strained but she attempted a smile. Frederick stumbled to his feet and managed an awkward bow. He could see her glance fitfully at his cheeks. The scars had not set as well as she might like, he guessed. She put on a smile, however, and extended her hand.

"How rude of you, sir," she said, "to not greet an old friend upon arrival. We have had a time of it getting here as well. I've told Fitton over and over we ought not to travel in the early spring, but he insisted it would be an insult to Lord Estibus were we not to come."

Frederick nodded and squeezed her hand. He meant it to be an apology squeeze (if that could be called a real thing), but it came off wrong. He hadn't touched her since their last meeting in the winter and her hand felt odd to him: meaty and strong compared to Isabella's thin delicate one. Perhaps memory had painted her oddly for him in her absence. He mumbled some niceties in response to her and took a long look at her face before moving on to shake Lord Fitton's hand and make an escape into other company. Her face had been tired

The card tables were arranged and set up for groups of four. Two would always be rotating in and out but as it would be a long night, into the morning hours, all would have plenty of time to play; that is, for those whose money held out. Frederick was quite relieved to be one of the odd men out on the first round. He would end at a table with Margery eventually but for now, he could escape onto the balcony for air and a smoke. Once out, he surveyed the obnoxious over-designed garden. His father had quite a few badly done Greek statues that lurked in the garden. In the moonlight, it looked as if armies hid in the bushes waiting to attack the house. Cuthbert had hated the garden when he was small, but Frederick would play in it, pretending he was among the armies and the house would soon be turned to rubble. A last chilly gust of clinging winter blew through the bushes, rushing through the newly sprung leaves. The old was not quite yet done with the new. He shivered as the gust, contained by the balcony, whirled around him. It also brought to him another scent of tobacco.

"The deuce!" he heard behind him while another match struck with more cursing.

"No cards this round for you, either?" said Frederick, going to Cuthbert and shielding the wind so his brother could light his cigarette.

"My thanks," said Cuthbert, taking a long draw and looking well sated. "That Kilkenny has got me for nigh on a hundred quid from cards at the club. I'm trying to avoid playing him again. I know he cheats."

"And you never cheat," said Frederick, staring at Cuthbert. He grumbled something unintelligible and waved away Frederick's comment. "Damned chilly out here, isn't it?"

"It's stuffy inside. I like this better."

"I see what you mean. Didn't know Father would be inviting them. He's thick as rocks when it comes to those sorts of things, but I suppose that's in your favor. Never noticed how you got on with that woman. A good thing, to be sure. Don't you relapse, now. It's a big house and I know things can be got away with, but Isabella is a good girl and you're lucky to have her."

Frederick rolled his eyes.

"You talk of Miss Fortridge and me as if it is a fixed thing," Frederick said. "Is it?"

"Well, hem, it well," Cuthbert occupied himself with fixing the roll of his smoke, though nothing appeared wrong with it. "Father and Fortridge seem to think so, but Isabella still reserves her right."

"She can still turn me down?" said Frederick, smiling to himself.

"Yes, she can," said Cuthbert, "but it seemed that she liked you. She's an optimistic one, that girl. She could make sunshine out of mud. I can't tell you what a value that is. My Lucy, good woman, good woman, but always clouds with her. Always something about the children, or the money, and though we stand to inherit, she worries that the inheritance will be too much trouble. Not enough money, too much money, more children. We have one damned near every year and they never stop crying. I'd like to not be worried every other moment."

Frederick wondered to himself if the children often went to the club, as that was where Cuthbert spent most of his time. So, he was to marry Isabella. It was certain. He could tell by the way his brother had hemmed and hawed. They decided things like that, about him, without consulting him. He never argued. It was always that way. It seemed Cuthbert had the decency to have some conscience about it this time. Frederick still said nothing. He stared at his brother, watching as Cuthbert cast about awkwardly for something else to say. He would soon give up and go in. His wife wouldn't stand him abandoning her for two rounds. Soon they were interrupted by someone else on the balcony. The light was behind them, but Frederick knew the form and turned away, back to the garden. Another chill breeze blew.

"Cuthbert," Margery said. "Lucy is looking for you. I'll sit out this round so you may play. Frederick, they've excused you again. I know how much you dislike lively company, so I begged you out. Cuthy, you'd better hurry, now there's a dear."

Cuthbert muttered but could say nothing to the call of his wife, who would come looking for him if he did not hurry. He glared at Frederick, but he would not turn around. He leaned on the railing gripping it, searching in the shrubs for his favorite statue: Poseidon, master of the seas. He had always been Frederick's general and Frederick his trusted strategist. He felt strongest when he had the power of the sea at his beck and call. He kept his mind on that as Margery clicked the door shut behind her. She was still outside. He could smell her jasmine.

"We ought to keep the chill out of the house," she said. She was right behind him now. He could feel her presence. He looked down over the edge of the balcony, wondering how far of a drop it was. Margery took a step closer and draped her arm over his shoulder and laid her cheek on his back. The tension went out of him at her touch like a reflex. She was going to be gentle tonight, but he didn't turn around. Frederick took another drag of his cigarette.

"You know, I don't mind it so much anymore," said Margery.

"What?" asked Frederick, pulling the words from his throat. It took all his energy to talk just now.

"The smell of the smoke. It reminds me of you now. Your father and those awful lawyers come to the house after their club and the reek of it trails in with them. They leave its miasma all over the halls. It's like you're there, but always around the corner where I can't touch you."

"Hmm." Frederick exhaled a long puffy trail and leaned back into Margery. He could feel the tension in her lessen and she wrapped her other arm around his chest like a mother welcoming a naughty child after the scolding was over. She thought she won but he was on a brink, teetering there with a cold wind threatening to blow him one way and a warm one the other.

"I met her, you know," said Margery, clutching his shirt a little.

"Isabella? So, you know?"

"Of course, I know. It's hardly a secret. Everything in line with normal happy tidings."

"What do you think of her?" Frederick asked, not quite knowing why he did.

"Ha! You want my opinion?" Margery said mirthlessly. "She's perfect, really. She's everything she ought to be and so expectant for life to give her everything. I ought to hate her but even I can't bring myself to do it. In fact, I'm happy she is what she is. Those kinds are the most oblivious. If we're careful, she'll never notice."

Frederick stiffened and paused with his cigarette halfway to his mouth. Isabella's face floated in front of him, smiling and rosy. She expected everything from him, but it was true, she would never notice. He turned to face Margery, still in her arms, their bodies close together.

A whiff of jasmine crept up between them and his body responded. She smirked up at him and pressed closer, making things worse. He could see her face now. She really was still beautiful.

This place felt familiar and safe. It was a small warm eddy in a cove away from the exhaustion of the others. He could still have this sanctuary, even though circumstances drifted him in other directions. But this warmth was only temporary, and he thought back to Isabella's kind words and bright face. It was not fire, but it was the warming rays of sunshine. Funny how he had not noticed until Cuthbert had pointed it out. That sun would dry him when this left him cold.

Frederick still stared down in Margery's face. She tilted her head back, ready to reconcile but Frederick could not bring himself to do it. Her arms felt like a trap now, rather than a comfort, and he pushed himself out of them. He leaned back out on the railing and looked to the garden. He spotted Poseidon.

"I can't," he said. "I want to give it a try. A real try."

"A try?" said Margery, reaching to grip his jacket.

"Yes. I've been given something good. I'm going to try in good faith."

"Faith?! Bah!" Margery gave him a flick on his chest. "You're trying anything. You're just letting your family decide your life again!"

"You just don't like it because you can't decide things," he spat back. Margery smacked him in the face. Frederick bit his lip and straightened his jacket.

"You ought to go back in," Frederick said. "You'll be missed soon."

"We'll both be missed," she said, smirking at him. "You wouldn't want your wife suspecting since you plan to give me up." Frederick said nothing. "I see you don't care," Margery said. "You've cut me, Frederick, really. I hope you're not so heartless to your new wife. I shan't forgive you, so don't expect to come creeping back when you've ruined things with her, or she's bored of your melancholy. I'm the only one who can really put up with it, you know."

Frederick tried to keep a straight countenance, but his face must have shown what he felt because Margery's smirk was the cruelest of all. With that, she caressed his breeches, leaving him in a state in which he could not go in for a moment. She flounced into the house and called out.

"Oh, Isabella, dear! I found him! He's out on the balcony. I tried to get him to come to you but he's being stubborn."

Bitch, thought Frederick, and quickly turned away from the light as the door opened. He hunched over the railing, looking down into the bushes below. Isabella peeked out timidly, and Frederick quickly finished off the smoke, tossing the butt over the edge. If he started a fire, he would have a reasonable excuse to go over the side.

"You didn't have to do that," said Isabella, coming up next to him and leaning over the rail. "I don't mind when men smoke."

"I was finished," said Frederick, glancing at her sideways. She turned to him and smiled. She left the door open and the light from inside showed her eyes twinkling. Her face was flushed, and he could only imagine how stuffy it had gotten in the room.

"Your brother sent me to find you," she said. "We're taking a break, but he said you'd better be in the next form. I saved you a spot in mine."

"You did?" He would have to play after all. It was probably for the best. Margery couldn't do much in company.

"Well," she began hesitantly. "Don't you think, um, I'm not sure, uh..."

TO MASTER THE TIDES

Frederick smiled at her but wasn't quite in a state to turn to her yet, especially as he would be facing the light. He coughed as an excuse to turn away and adjust. The ridiculousness of it was enough to remedy the situation and he could turn his attention to her.

"No need to stand on ceremony with me, of all people," he said. "We'll need to talk of it sooner or later." His frankness was a farce, but it seemed to give her courage. He claimed he wanted openness, but he would never tell her what had happened a moment ago. Still, if he could come to some easiness with her, so much the better."

"Don't you think we ought to spend as much time as possible getting to know one another?" Isabella said in a rush. "We've such a short time to talk and if we're to be married and, um, all that goes with it, I want to be sure all is right beforehand."

"You're reconciled to me then?" asked Frederick.

"My father has it all arranged," said Isabella. "You seem like such a kind man, but what if I'm not the right one for you? I've heard of these things, where families arrange things, and someone is in love with another, and it's doomed from the start."

"I'm not in love with anyone," Frederick said, "if that's what you're worried about." He wondered at the conviction in his voice. It was there for Margery. He realized it like a shock. She was familiar but he didn't love her and was indignant at her insistence to always be there. He wasn't her toy, and he wouldn't be. "I'm not in love with anyone," said Frederick again, softening his tone to look Isabella in the eye. She seemed as if she had a question on her lips but instead ignored his behavior.

"What about you?" asked Frederick, almost as an afterthought. "I'm not keeping you from anyone, am I?"

"No," said Isabella, smiling. "You're not, but I'm glad you care. I'm free as the wind, though I wish this wind were a little warmer!"

"Would you like my jacket?"

"No, I'll bear it. I can bear most things! I'm not that fragile, you know. My father seems to think I am. But we ought to get back in. They'll be waiting on us to start."

Frederick nodded and gave Isabella his arm.

Inside, the tables awaited them. Cuthbert was at one with his wife Lucy, and based on the two empty chairs, that was where Frederick and Isabella were to join. Margery was entertaining Lord Estibus and his club friends. Their wives and the Weathertons were bent over their cards, brows wrinkled. He could hear Margery laughing and losing splendidly. Those amid the serious match cast intermittent scalding glances at her, but she laughed all the more. Frederick angled his back against her, but he could feel her eyes on the back of his neck. Isabella took the seat next to Lucy and the two giggled at the other tables.

"I believe the Whethertons are down nearly 50 pounds each," whispered Lucy, with a mock scandalized tone in her voice. "The lawyers' wives are regular sharks."

"Come, Frederick," Cuthbert said. "You shan't get out of any more games. The Fortridges have gone home for the night, so we are at even numbers."

"Oh!" Isabella said. "Am I to stay here this evening?!"

"Yes," Cuthbert said. "Your parents have entrusted you to us. We will see you home if you like but there are plenty of fresh rooms."

"Entrusted her to me, you mean," said Lucy, dealing out the cards. "I believe Mr. Fortridge said he only trusted you as far as he could sniff your farts and not even then."

Cuthbert grumbled again and Frederick sniggered. Isabella turned bright red.

"I do wish father wouldn't say such things," she said, hiding behind her cards. "I do wonder at him in his old age."

They began the game. Isabella proved to be wretched. Frederick, ahead of her in the deal, tried to be merciful but still, she made poor decisions. Cuthbert, on the other hand, took advantage of her every misstep and snatched up each opportunity to show her up. She tried to play it off with a laugh, but Cuthbert insisted on crowing. Worse, he did so under the guise of instructing Isabella.

"Now, really," Lucy said after Isabella had receded into silence. "Why must you punish her so? This is all to be in good fun."

"Well, how will she ever learn with my foolish brother feeding her cards the whole time?" he asked.

"You were?" said Isabella turning to Frederick. He coughed but did not answer. Her face looked even more pained. She turned to Lucy and grabbed her arm. "Do you think everyone was doing that?"

"Don't worry about it, dear," said Lucy. "It's only a game. Cuthbert would do well to remember it."

"It's all right," Isabella said, though clearly it wasn't. "Our round is done, isn't it? I know at least that much. You'll excuse me. I'm a little tired of cards. I'll just go sit in there for a moment." Isabella stumbled to her feet and bumped into the table and her chair in a flustered rush and headed out of the room.

"You ass," said Frederick, under his breath. "Ought I to go after her?" he asked Lucy.

"No, Cuthbert should," she said. "He needs to apologize."

Cuthbert did as he was told and a few moments later, they came back to the party. Isabella came in first, a little flushed from crying. She took a long look at Frederick from across the room, put on a smile, and went to him. Cards were done for the night as the Whethertons had lost all their money. Someone called for dancing and one of the maids was awakened to play for them. It was well past two in the morning before all was said and done. Isabella had cheered up considerably after having found Frederick was an excellent dance partner and was still lively late into the night even though she drooped not a little from want of sleep.

There was a shuffling at the door when it was time to leave. As it ended, the Fittons were to take Isabella home and Frederick could not protest it without drawing attention. Isabella seemed to have taken a liking to Margery and they walked out arm in arm. Before they went out the door, with Margery whispering nonstop in Isabella's ear, she suddenly turned to Frederick with an inscrutable look on her face. It soon cracked and she smiled broadly and waved to him.

"Come to see me tomorrow!" she said. "If you're not too tired."

Frederick was surprised at this and found himself waving dumbly in return.

Four

Frederick did see Isabella the next day and many days after that. The strangeness of their first encounter soon wore off in the boring comfort of normalcy. They never talked about their betrothal. Their visits consisted of chaperoned sittings and talks of the weather. Occasionally, they walked to town with her parents for tea, but then it was too hot for that, or it rained for a week straight and the roads were muck. Things progressed in this fashion for several months and then all of a sudden— it seemed to Frederick—they were married.

The ceremony was held in the tiny country church in the dead heat of summer. Isabella fainted at the end of it and Frederick nearly missed catching her. They excused themselves early from the wedding breakfast and took refuge in the cooler end of the house shaded by the forest that abutted Frederick's uncle's home, now his. He'd been in possession only a month. He'd waited on purpose. He didn't want the place to feel like home until Isabella could come. He was afraid if he got used to it without her, she would never belong. Now was the true test.

There was a heavy downpour on the wedding night, well after all the guests had gone home and the evening had cooled considerably. Frederick was thankful for it and he threw open all the windows in his room to take in the rain-soaked air, even though the wind threatened to put out the candles. His uncle never bothered with the gas lights, even now when most of his set flirted with electricity.

Frederick liked the candlelight, especially now with the rain. He had always loved the smell of a storm. He was tempted to step onto the balcony and let the hot rain soak him through but just then Isabella came to him.

She stood in the doorway in her long dressing gown tied up to her neck. She was lit by the oil lamp she carried, and her long braid hung over her shoulder. She absently twisted it around and around between her fingers. Frederick turned to her. He hadn't finished undressing. His shirt was undone and his chest bare. Isabella went to him at the window, staring at the hair on his chest. She reached up to touch it but then pulled her hand back.

"I had no idea men had hairy chests," she said.

"That's what you're amazed at?" said Frederick, wondering what else she didn't know.

"Oh, don't worry," she said, trying to sound confident. "I've been told what to expect." She gritted her teeth and stuck out her lower lip. Frederick tried not to laugh but she saw what he was feeling. "Don't," she said, indignant. "I'm sure all women are the same at first. No one wants to tell us anything, no matter how much we ask. Don't you think that's foolish? We'll all find out eventually, or were they worried I would be an old maid and should never know?"

"I doubt you would've been an old maid even if you hadn't married me," said Frederick, stepping a little closer to Isabella. She had set down her lamp on the table by the window and it shone behind her, creating a silhouette of her body. She was a thin little thing, smaller than he expected; he hoped he wouldn't damage her. He looked down on her and could see she was nervous. She wasn't trembling, though, and she met his glaze with courage. He paused for a moment. He meant to take her in one quick embrace but what was this for her? What was she feeling? This wasn't some passion as he felt in the past. This was duty. It gave him reservations, but it had to be done. She was here and determined. It would shame her to send her away.

He leaned down and kissed her. Her lips were cold and small, and her hair smelled of a fresh wash. He pulled her in close and his arms enveloped her much more than he expected. His body responded to her and he could feel a cautious hand reach down, then pull back.

"Go ahead, if you want," he said. And she reached down and took a firm hold. "A little gentler than that," he said between kisses. But her curious fingers were nearly too much for him. His kisses became more ardent, and it wasn't very long before he took her to his bed.

Isabella had her back to him when it was all through. Frederick reached out a hesitant hand and touched the ivory skin of her back. He felt the tension slip out of her as he touched her. Encouraged, he pulled her in close and she nestled into him.

"I'm glad," said Isabella.

"For what," asked Frederick.

"I thought you wouldn't comfort me after."

"Was it so bad that you needed comforting?"

"No," said Isabella. "I was told that it might hurt but it was nothing like what I thought. Was it what you thought? I mean, not me, but in general, the first time."

"Not exactly, um."

"It's all right," said Isabella, turning towards him with a gleam in her eye, like a child that's done something naughty. "Margery's told me everything."

"What?" said Frederick, sitting up. "What has she told you?"

"About men," she said, voice catching a little in her throat. "About how their fathers takes them to one of *those* houses for their first time and how, how it all works. You look positively horrified that I know. Was it wrong of me to find out before our wedding night?"

"No, of course not," said Frederick. His heart was taking its time sliding back down from his throat, but he laid back down, his arm across his forehead. "Are you and Lady Fitton on such intimate terms, then?"

"I wouldn't go that far," said Isabella. "Something about her doesn't seem quite proper but one can talk to her about things, without being afraid of being laughed at or gasped at. That's what my mother did when I asked about it. And my city cousins, they're much faster there, you know; they simply snickered and called me a child. Margery took me seriously and I am grateful for that."

"You shouldn't associate with her so much," Frederick said. "As you said, she's not quite proper."

"Who am I to associate with, then?" asked Isabella. "She's my only acquaintance here."

"We'll make the rounds," said Frederick. "And my father's sure to invite his whole set once the shooting season starts. You were good friends with Cuthbert's wife in town, were you not?"

"Yes, I was," she said. Frederick wondered for a moment at the strange smile on her face but let it pass.

TO MASTER THE TIDES

They never did "make the rounds," as Frederick had promised, though a few women paid the obligatory calls to Isabella. As a result, after six months of marriage, Isabella knew relatively few of the families in the neighborhood. She did her best to entertain, though many of the niceties seemed to be lost on the country folk. She never said a word, but he could often hear the exasperation in her voice when trying to converse with the other women. None of them read novels nor kept up with the latest gossip outside their small town. Though Frederick had done his best to remedy the passage to their home, the way was still difficult, and Isabella could not entertain as much as she wished.

"I do wish you'd come with me to visit once in a while," said Isabella, as she was leaving for tea. "I always promise you'll be there next time, and I'm tired of making excuses. It is not as if you are busy."

Frederick couldn't argue. He was sitting by the fire, still in his dressing gown, a scone in one hand and a book in the other. He had seldom been to the stables since they'd been married and left everything to his steward.

"What have I to say to any of them?" he asked. "Things never change here. You say so yourself."

"It would be nice if you would show some support for your wife," said Isabella.

"Don't be such a nag, dear," said Frederick, staring at the lines on the page but not reading them. He kept his eyes fixed there until Isabella was gone. The door slammed and Frederick sighed. He didn't wish to make Isabella's life so boring, but why couldn't she do things without him? Is that what marriage was? He should have followed the path of his uncle and remained alone. What did he expect to happen? The passion he had felt with Margery? Now that that was long cold, he could see it was an addiction, but it didn't stop him from craving it all the more. It used to be only thing that made him wish to get out of bed in the mornings, but that feeling was gone. What if she was the only one who could bring that fire and it was now lost forever? He'd felt a spark with Isabella in the beginning and had hoped for it, longed for it, but soon realized his attentions were stifling to her. She only cared about his presence and appearance to others. When they were at home alone, he might as well be invisible.

Perhaps he ought to do something with himself. Anything. He went to his room and dressed. Some days he never did. He didn't see the point before dinner. Today, he did dress, though. He put on some rough boots and working clothes. He would go out to the stables today. He always had looked forward to working with the horses once he knew he was to inherit them but had yet to go out to them more than twice. He hoped the stableman would recognize him.

It was a longer walk than he'd remembered, and he was quite winded when he got there. He saw the gamekeeper's cottage, the same one he could see from his father's estate, and realized it was much closer than he had thought. It seemed well cared for at a closer glance and the trail of smoke coming from the chimney made it seem a comforting sort of place. The keeper would be taking a trip soon to visit his daughter. The steward would look after the cottage. Frederick fancied perhaps he would look after the cottage. He could hide there for the week and bring a pile of books. No one would bother him to go visiting or attend church. Isabella could do the house as she liked and invite whoever she liked for dinner and be free of him.

It was mildly satisfying to him to realize how much Isabella might enjoy his absence. She could invite Margery and the two could abuse him as they pleased. They talked about all things, apparently. The last time Isabella was in his bed, she had wound her fingers in his hair and pulled his head back to bite his neck. Margery used to do that. Should he be appalled with himself that he had imagined Margery in her place and turned more forceful as he had been with his former lover? Perhaps. Isabella had been more distant after that and not done the thing again.

When Frederick reached the stables, the stableman was glad to see him. He worked with his sons to do the mucking and carrying; few others were around to talk to during the day. Frederick, though, enjoyed talking of horses and hearing about the new filly that was nearly ready to ride. She'd been foaled in the spring and was as gentle as could be. Frederick smiled at the sight of her, a lovely creamy butter color with a white patch on her nose.

"She was an accident," the stableman said, "when the new stud got loose. No good for breeding, but she is quiet and sweet as can be. Mrs. Estibus might take her for a ride now and then. She needs some exercise. The horse, I mean, sir, not your wife. I'm sure your wife is fair well."

"She could use some exercise, too," Frederick said. If Isabella were tired, she might leave him alone. He patted the little horse's nose affectionately, thinking he should come to the stables more. The horse looked at him with soft brown eyes and nuzzled his neck.

"I ought to come out here more," he said to the stableman. "You said the stud got out?"

"We need more hands, to be sure. Your uncle wanted to start breeding and brought in men here and there, but we'll need a man or two permanent if you want to keep with his plans."

"I'll keep an eye out and ask around at church," he said, patting the filly. "When will she be ready to ride?"

"She's just broke but I'd say she could take a new rider. She's so quiet she'd bear just about anything."

Frederick felt a renewed spring in his step as he went back to the house. The air was a little crisp with the nearness of fall. He wondered why he'd neglected the stables in the first place. It was a project, something to occupy his mind. He would present Isabella with the horse and tell her about it tonight. He ought to be better about the social aspects of life as well. He knew that and though they wore on him dreadfully, it wasn't right to make Isabella suffer and miss them when she relied on them so much for amusement. He would make it right.

Frederick took a deep breath and looked up to the sky before he went inside. It was still blue. How long since he'd remembered that? Things would be well. This new vigor would last this time. He would make her a present and she'd care for him again. He'd do better taking her to meet people as well and it would all be as she'd hoped. He turned the handle of his front door and went in.

Frederick was greeted by his servant who took his dirty work coat between thumb and forefinger. Frederick apologized profusely for the smell of the stables and asked if Isabella was home yet. He was informed that she was in the sitting room and Lady Fitton had just taken her leave.

The front door closed, and the room went exceedingly dark as his eyes had not yet adjusted from the bright sunlight. He was in his home again and its familiar feel took over his brief recovery at the stables. That feeling was seeping out of him too quickly to grasp and he didn't try. He went to Isabella in the sitting room. She sat in front of the fireplace, reading a letter. She started when she heard Frederick come in and crumpled the letter in her hands. The look on her face was inscrutable. As blank as could be but holding in something.

"Is something the matter?" he asked, pausing in his own emotion to indulge in curiosity. It was a welcome relief, in fact, from his confusion. The more the feeling he had outside faded the more he grew numb again. "Did something in the letter trouble you?"

"What?! This?" Isabella quickly threw the note on the fire. "Just some rot from an acquaintance in town. The information in there has nothing, nothing to do with the life I live. How can he even presume? Makes things ever the more complicated ..."

"Isabella?" he said. She glanced at him as if she'd forgotten he was there. "Where have you been all this time?"

"I've been at the stables," he said. "A new little horse that was born in the spring is just broke. She's a sweet thing. I thought you might like her to ride."

"Ride?" Isabella said. "It's nearly winter! How am I to ride down that blasted hill?"

"We might go into the city and stay at the townhouse."

"If I could believe you, that might be all well and good. You never think of me. You only say what you think I want to hear then go on your merry way. If you were always at the club or a drunk or a gambling man, perhaps I could make excuses, that if you only could master your devils, you'd be everything you should be. But no, you are simply lazy and a fool, dreaming away with your books and doing nothing."

"I did go to the stables today," he said. "I thought you might like the new horse."

"I hate horses!" Isabella got to her feet and went to the liquor cabinet. She whipped open the door and poured herself a fat brandy. "If you'd ever ask me questions rather than sit silently you might know that. I hate your books. I can't see what practical use could be made of philosophy or any of that rot you read all day. You spend all your time thinking about things that don't matter. It would have been best you never married. You haven't even noticed I'm a drunk!" She downed her brandy and filled the glass again. Her eyes were swimming with liquor and anger.

"I rarely look in the cabinet," said Frederick, at a loss as to what he should say. He went over to Isabella who still clung to the bottle. Her eyes flashed as he approached. What did she expect him to do? Whatever it was, he had disappointed her again. He took the bottle from her hand and poured himself a measure.

"I wish I were a drunk," he said. "At least then there would be some escape from all this."

"From me?"

"No." He waved his hand to indicate the room, the house, the world, he wasn't sure exactly what. "All of it. Life. The human condition."

Isabella rolled her eyes.

TO MASTER THE TIDES

"There you go on again," she said. "You can never handle the specifics. I want to go out! I want to have friends! I'm bored of this. I'm bored of you coming to my room. I'm sick to death of ..." she hesitated and for a moment and Frederick almost thought she looked frightened, but he only looked up at her with half-closed eyes. The brandy on an empty stomach was already clouding his wits. "I'm sick to death of my duty."

"Oh," was all he said.

"You don't care?" said Isabella hesitantly.

"It's been six months and we've no sign of children," he said. "Haven't you suspected that something must be wrong with one of us? What else is that good for between us, at any rate?"

"No," she said, quiet at last. "I hadn't thought."

"If you want to go out, go out," said Frederick. "I don't intend to impede your happiness. That was never my intent. I'm not sure I had any intent at all."

"I shall go out," said Isabella, regaining some spirit. "Margery said I may stay with her whenever the weather makes it too difficult to come home."

Frederick opened his mouth but closed it again. He vaguely thought he ought to insist against the further intimacy of the two but what right had he to say? He thought it likely the county all knew about his affair with Lady Fitton. Isabella would be laughed at but what would it matter if she never knew and fancied herself to be having fun? He would leave her to it. He was done concerning himself with her.

"Do as you please," said Frederick, downing the last of his brandy and, taking the bottle, stalked out of the room.

Five

Frederick ended up in his study, though he wasn't sure how. He felt he had wandered around the house for some time. The bottle of brandy was still clutched in his fist and he set it down hard on his writing desk. He sat down and laid his head in his hands, fingers clenched in his hair. He watched the light of the fireplace dance through the brown liquor. The servants were very good at keeping the fires lit and the house warm. Was that Isabella's doing, or did they simply know their jobs? Did it matter? He couldn't remember what it was like before. He moved to the place in the summer, and it was too hot for fires that year, even at night. Did it matter? Any of it?

Frederick began thinking *those* thoughts again but in a meandering way, similar to how he walked to his office. He felt warm inside, but he knew it to be the artificial warmth of the liquor. He didn't like it and fought to pull his thoughts straight, but it was like trying to see underwater. He desperately willed himself not to be drunk but that, of course, was impossible. He laid his head on the desk and gave in to his thoughts. Once he decided, *Yes, I will let myself think that*, it became all he thought of.

I suppose I really am useless. Useless to her. If she had not married me, perhaps she should have married someone better. Perhaps that was who the letter was from. Someone who has stomach for company and trifling books. What was Cuthbert about, tying the poor thing to our family? And I suppose I am useless to this house, not filling it with a family. Cuthbert has several sons. One of them could inherit one day. The servants keep the place warm without my lifting a finger. I really am useless. Better to drink myself into oblivion.

Frederick swirled the liquor around in the bottle and decided that would be a very bad plan. He was already a burden on everyone and death in that fashion would be slow and wearisome to those around him. He thought of the poor little horse in the stables with no one to ride her. Cuthbert would see the horses were taken care of properly. Frederick failed at even that. He could have hired someone else; he just never had gotten around to doing so. It was his fault nothing had gone the way he hoped. He neglected the stables. He neglected his wife. He had nothing. He had a mistress if he wanted her but Margery had likely moved on. The only good thing he had and he ruined it. He was a useless, useless thing, no good for even a bored old woman's toy.

And finally, Frederick turned *that* thought loose. What if he were to do it? He never let himself think about it before. It was the coward's way out, or was it? He found himself thinking of Hamlet and how the pitiful Dane worked himself up to believe it might be braver to face the unknown. No, it was the coward's excuse and simple masturbation of the ego. But one must justify all things done if they are a man. A man's decision is final.. Frederick laughed out loud at his thoughts. *What is it to be a man? To go forth bravely and let no other tell him he is wrong? Perhaps I am not a man, but a coward and a dog. So be it. I am a cur, then, and no use to anyone.*

JOSEPHINE BORGIA

Frederick stood and steadied himself a moment, his head swimming from his decision nearly as much as the alcohol. He rummaged through his desk until he found the pistols that had been his uncle's. They were meant for dueling but at close range, one could do damage enough. He loaded one and grabbed the bottle of brandy in case he lost his resolve. He would become dead drunk and then he would do it. It was time.

Frederick was glad he met no servants as he stamped out the front door of his house. He didn't look back. There would be no final looks or words to his wife. He left no note. What good was all that, anyway? To say he loved her? He hadn't and she had not loved him. They shared some furtive nights but even she had lost all joy in those. He knew that early on. He never forced himself on her but in his heart, he knew she hadn't wanted him there. It was nearly as bad, and it made him quicken his pace.

In some unconscious moment, he decided to head for the gamekeeper's cottage. The moon shone bright, and he could easily keep his direction. He fancied he could see the reflection glint off the windows of the tiny place. He knew the keeper to be away visiting a daughter. If somehow his aim went awry, there would be no one to help him. It would be slow and painful but there would be no backing out. It would be over at last and Isabella would be free at least. He took solace in that. Perhaps the letter had been from a disappointed lover. Cuthbert would see she got a healthy sum of Frederick's money and then perhaps she could do as she pleased. He should have told her intrigues were permissible, but her sensibilities might not have allowed that. It would all be right now at any rate.

TO MASTER THE TIDES

Why worry over such trifles? The wind whipped up and gave him a chill. He took another swig of brandy from the bottle to reinstate the effects that had worn down in the cold.

Frederick's walk was longer than he anticipated. At first, he set off as on a lark, some silly thing he wanted to do as he and his classmates had done in school. Now it was more a determination. *It is all for the good*, he repeated to himself over and over as he stomped through the fields. His nose and fingertips began to chill, and he wished he had brought a lantern, but it didn't matter if he found the place, did it? He could do the thing here if need be. But then he heard a noise. It was far off and carried on the wind. He could hear it now and then when it blew in the right direction, but he could not make out what it was. Sometimes it sounded like a yell of a woman. Other times it sounded like the grunting of men. Perhaps it was the other lost souls coming to meet him early. He pushed forward towards the cottage. Before long he could tell that the sounds were earthly.

The moonlight, now at its zenith, crept out from behind a cloud and lit the ground in front of the cabin. Struggling in the dirt were two men, fighting tooth and nail. Frederick stood there, pistol and brandy at his sides, for a good minute before he got a clear listen to the voices of the men. Amid the swearing, he realized one of them was his steward. Without thinking, he aimed the pistol in the air and fired. This got the men's attention and the two fell off each other and scrabbled away in the dirt. Frederick held the pistol in close in hopes they wouldn't notice it was the type to only have one shot.

"Mr. Estibus!" said the steward, quickly getting to his feet. "Thanks to God you're here. This man here, I found wandering on the property. Before I could ask him any questions, he was on me."

The other man got to his feet. He was tall and well-built as far as Frederick could tell in the dark and it was a wonder to him that his stocky steward had been holding his own. He wondered what he ought to do and was about to question the man when a woman's scream came from the cabin. It was a blood-curdling sound and it made Frederick's stomach turn.

"Who is that?" asked the steward. "What's wrong with her?!"

Frederick took a step forward, sticking the pistol in the large man's stomach, taking care to keep it in the dark.

"My wife," said the man looking Frederick in the eye. The man knew he wouldn't shoot even had the gun been capable.

"I see," said Frederick, looking right back. "You were protecting your wife. McCaulty, go at once for a doctor. She does not seem well."

McCaulty looked as if he wanted to protest but the woman screamed again, and the steward ran off with a hop toward the stables.

"What is the matter?" asked Frederick, sticking the pistol in his waistband. The man glared at him. Frederick could understand that he might not want his affairs meddled in, but he was on Estibus land, after all. Frederick pushed his question.

"Baby," said the man. He looked down at the pistol and snickered. "Name's Miller."

"I see," said Frederick. Miller looked dirty and poor. Perhaps they were traveling and had no choice. Frederick considered him a moment. He didn't look as if he were going to cause any more trouble so Frederick handed Miller the brandy bottle. He took a long drink. His scowl did not lessen but his shoulders relaxed, and Frederick felt they had come to an uneasy truce. The woman in the cottage screamed again.

"Shouldn't you go to her?" Frederick asked. "There will be no one else to disturb you and the doctor isn't that far."

"Leave her be," Miller said.

"She might be dying."

Miller said nothing. The woman screamed again. Frederick hesitated a moment, then darted into the cabin.

Inside, it was dark, with the moon being almost directly overhead. A tiny woman with an overgrown belly, impossibly large for her small frame, lay flat, panting on the cot, blood everywhere. The smell of it made Frederick wince and gag, but he pushed forward to the side of the bed. What could he do until the doctor arrived? He ripped off his jacket and wadded it in a ball. He lifted her by her shoulders and stuffed it under her head.

"Can you breathe a little better now?" he asked. He thought she nodded, and her panting grew a little easier. "Forgive me," said Frederick. "I'm not sure what else to do." He looked to Miller who stood in the doorway. The man took another drink of the brandy. Frederick turned to the woman. Sweat covered her brow and he could tell she wanted to scream again but instead, she bit down on a sleeve of his jacket. It pained him to see her trying so hard. He groped for her arm until he found her hand and grabbed it. He didn't look to the man. If he'd wanted to come to his wife, he would have by now. Frederick wasn't about to ask permission for this.

"Squeeze when it hurts," he said to her. "Break it if you must." He, of all people, deserved to feel pain. He was selfish, useless, and immoral. He couldn't believe this tiny creature was any of these things. She clasped her fingers through his immediately and he was surprised how delicate yet strong they were. Fragile, yet crushing his bones without issue. They sat there for what seemed like forever in the dark of night, the moon slowly moving, bit by bit adding rays of light to the room. Long moments passed, punctuated by intense moments of pain, but the woman didn't scream out again. Frederick made no grunt himself; he ought not to complain while she endured so much. And out of sync with all of that was the swishing of the brandy in the bottle as Miller took another drink.

The moon moved again, almost too fast, it seemed to Frederick. Perhaps it wanted to show him something. The light shone through the window now and fell on the woman's face. It was heart-shaped, and her eyes were light brown, almost golden. They stared directly at him, open wide, strained, and determined. He stared back and between them, there was an understanding. He would not leave her, and she would be strong. She would make it through. Nothing mattered but what was between them at the moment, an animal-like recognition of another breathing being, bereft of any walls erected by polite company. Blood, skin, touch, and sweat were all allowed and not vulgar things. He would lend himself to her and she would use him.

The spell was broken when Dr. Archer and McCaulty made a noisy entrance. The moon slipped along its path and the light was gone. Frederick still clutched the woman's hand.

"The hell?!" Archer said when he came on the scene. "Should have called a mid-wife for this!"

TO MASTER THE TIDES

"Mr. Estibus told me ..." McCaulty said, hands wringing.

"Never mind now," said Archer, who had started unpacking his satchel despite the scolding. "All you damned men get out."

Miller and McCaulty retreated without argument, but Frederick only stared. The doctor eyed his hand clasped with the woman's and pursed his lips but said nothing. He waved his hand to signal Frederick to turn around if he must stay. Barking quick orders at McCaulty to bring hot water, and linen among other things, he went to work.

Frederick barely registered anything that happened over the rest of the night. Everything was muffled around him and his eyes only saw what was directly in front, as one feels when they are about to pass out from being overheated. All that there was for him was her. The moon had continued on its path and no longer illuminated her face but still, that's all he focused on. There were cycles of pain and labored breathing; but now and then she was focused on him and he on her. In those moments all that existed to Frederick were the two of them and they existed as only flesh and blood and nothing else; no names, no stations, simply lonely animals wandering the earth, connected somehow in this impossible moment.

Time passed, though Frederick didn't feel as if it should have. The woman screamed one last time, and Archer barked more orders. Frederick followed them as best he could in his detached way until the woman had dropped his hand and fell back on the bed, panting heavily. He went to her, ignoring Archer who was still barking at him. She didn't look at Frederick. The spell between them was broken now though Frederick was still searching for it. The shrill cry of the infant jerked him back to reality as the doctor shoved the baby into his arms.

"Clean her up," Archer said. "I have to tend to the mother."

Frederick goggled at the doctor, bloody sleeves rolled up, hair wild, and back at the woman, sprawled awkwardly across the cot, too exhausted to get into a more comfortable position. Frederick stood there, the baby held awkwardly in his palms, the little thing wailing away heartily.

"Wake up, Estibus!" Archer bellowed. "You can't just stand there. Clean her up and get her warm!"

In a daze, Frederick went to the tub of water, holding the child like some pottery that was on the verge of falling to pieces. He looked down at her, and finally registered what he was holding. He could not take his eyes off her. Frederick had never seen a newborn before. All his nieces and nephews were many months old before he visited them. This little thing was tiny and nearly fit into one meaty palm and he couldn't stop staring at her squirming and fussing. Taking up a towel, he held her close, gently cleaning her tiny arm, each little finger, and toe, and soon enough, he was laughing stupidly at the wonder of her and found his eyes full of tears. Why was he crying? He hadn't even cried when his mother died. He never felt anything. And now he felt so much he couldn't contain it and it all came out in a muddle, completely out of his control.

"It's a baby!" he said stupidly to the doctor, holding up the child.

"What?" said Archer, wiping his brow distractedly and continuing to work on the woman. "Of course, it is. Wrap her up, at least."

TO MASTER THE TIDES

Frederick did as he was told and, plunking down in the middle of the floor, held the baby close as if the world were coming for her. He wouldn't let that happen, though. The baby fussed but was swaddled fairly well in the linen. She was probably wanting milk. Frederick looked to the mother who was still lying back, only half-conscious. He looked around for Miller next, calling out to him when the man wasn't readily apparent.

"He's gone off," said McCaulty, sticking his head in the door. "He was quite drunk, finished the brandy. He stumbled off, though I doubt he's still going in the same direction as he started inasmuch as he was stumbling and weaving. We'll probably need to search the fields in the morning."

"Do you think he left for good?" asked Frederick. He felt a pang for the little girl in his arms.

"I doubt it. He'll remember himself in the morning, I'll wager."

Frederick wasn't so sure. He made a note to himself to put together a search party.

"She can take the baby now," said the doctor. "C'mon now, Estibus, did you think you'd get to keep her?"

"Oh? Oh, all right," Frederick said, in a daze. He went over to where the woman was, still looking like death, but the doctor had cleaned her up and replaced linens as best he could. The woman now had an air of dignity in her exhaustion, although Frederick thought still much too pale. The woman had her arms outstretched and was smiling as she took her baby.

Frederick sat down again on the floor and leaned against the far wall, hanging his head. He felt he ought not to watch the woman feed her child. He had been up all night and was fast feeling the effects of the alcohol, but he was wide awake; too awake, he thought. What would happen now? Of course, he wouldn't keep the baby! What was the doctor about? What would happen to them? Did they have jobs? Where were they going? The poor little thing. What would become of her? She declared wholeheartedly that she was here when she came crying into the world. She was so small yet already so determined to live. She would have to fight hard for that, and it was the very thing he earlier determined he had no use for.

"What should I name her?" asked the woman. Her voice rolled in like a gentle tide on the rocks. He very nearly could feel the cool spray on his face like the time his mother took him to the seaside. "It is a kind tide today," she had said.

"Abigail," said Frederick.

"Oh?" the woman said. "It's a nice name."

"It was my mother's.

Six

Months went by and then years. Frederick did not see the woman or her husband in all that time. He soon forgot her amid all the dinner parties and trips to London. He did his best to keep Isabella happy, though she only drank more. He could do nothing to stop her friendship with Margery Fitton, so he let it be. Either Margery never said anything about him, or Isabella didn't care. Either was likely.

The stableman tired of waiting for Frederick to come down and hired a man or two. They all knew their business and he left them to it. The horses were exercised and cared for and bred. The estate made money and Frederick never lifted a finger. He only floated along. He vaguely wondered what happened to the little butter horse he got for Isabella. She never rode her and only took the carriage. He would check when he got back.

Frederick was in town today. It was cold for March and nothing had budded yet. Everything looked gray, the dirt, the buildings. Even the congested carriages up and down the cobblestone streets. It threatened rain. Frederick walked amongst the crowd on the sideways and pulled up the collar on his portmanteau to shield his neck from the wind. The weather had started to spit. He ought to get indoors, but he had no destination in mind. He headed to his club.

JOSEPHINE BORGIA

The club was just as crowded as the streets. He nodded at a few men as he came in and fished his copy of "De Anima" from his pocket as the valet took the coat. Dodging the people he knew, he found a set near a fire, ordered some scotch, and stuck his nose in his book.

The lines of the book blurred together. It was an argument he had read nearly a hundred times and didn't care for anymore.

He took to staring about the room, mind blank. The woodwork, the paintings, the men and their cigarette smoke, it all choked him. He let himself think *those* thoughts again. He hadn't in some time. Not since the night he went to the gamekeeper's cabin. Oh yes. That. How had he forgotten that? What became of the woman? What was her name? It didn't matter. But that moment. That one moment, when he looked her in the eye. That was more real than his entire life. Did the child survive? Frederick left his copy of Aristotle on the side table and left the club.

Next, Frederick went for coffee at the sweet shop next to the milliners. Margery liked the biscuits from that shop. The shop was meant for ladies, everything done up with frills and flowers. The bright colors of the petals on the walls looked dull in the muted sunlight from outside. A few candles were lit, and the shop was a little smoky.

Frederick sat at a high table by the window and chewed on a biscotti. He watched the people in the room, ladies bent over their tea and biscuits, giggling together in quiet confidence. Every now and then, a lady would cast a worried glance at someone else in the shop. *Did she hear me? No? Well, let me tell you this!*

TO MASTER THE TIDES

Frederick sipped his coffee, but no one noticed him. It was as if he was behind a veil, in his own world. When he had gone behind it, he couldn't tell. It was not at the club; people saw him there. The valet handed him his coat. On the street, someone tried to chase him down to return his book. He smiled wide and said it was a donation to the club. He had read it enough, too much, perhaps.

The smile was a veil itself, but this was different. His smile was painful, no matter how it looked on the outside. Where he was now, was comforting. His coffee warmed him, and he could look about at his ease. He stopped thinking about what should be done for Isabella or the horses. He was content. It was an odd feeling. Everyone around him faded into the background. He stared out the window of the shop. The sun was coming out, peeping through the clouds, showing off stripes of blue. People had their coats and cloaks strung across their arms as they walked by.

A woman and a little girl passed the shop. Frederick might never have picked them out had the girl not paused and stared up at him. She was about five or six, with curly white-blond hair and pale cheeks. What made Frederick take notice, however, was her bright green eyes, brighter than the grass. *Fairy eyes*, he thought.

The girl paused and gave him a good stare and the mother tugged her along. The mother looked at Frederick to see why the girl stopped. Her eyes and Frederick's met. He tried to smile at her, but he was still behind the veil and there were no false smiles in the veil. He nodded instead. Other people passed in front of the woman and child and they were gone.

JOSEPHINE BORGIA

The incident left Frederick a bit disconcerted. He had met the woman before. He had seen those eyes—the eyes of a lonely animal wandering the earth. It couldn't be. It couldn't. Frederick leaped to his feet, knocking over his stool. The clatter tore down the veil and all the ladies in the coffee shop turned his way, chatter suspended. He made a hasty apology and dashed out the door.

Out in the crowd, he had no idea which way the woman might have gone. Had she continued on her way or melted into the crowd? Did she recognize him or was she staring at the odd man in the ladies' coffee shop? She likely thought him a ponce. It didn't matter if she did, but he wanted to know about her. Or did he? He stopped at the edge of the street. Anonymous people milled about in all directions. The sun was out, and the veil was gone. So were the woman and the child, the lost Fae and the Fairy girl, denizens of the veil world. He would leave them there for now.

"What are you doing standing about like a dunce!" Cuthbert walked up to him and poked at Frederick's ankle with his cane. "Come with me to the club. You can stare absently in there and no one will think twice about it."

"Already been there." But he followed Cuthbert, anyway.

The brothers returned to the club and settled in with some cigars. Frederick hated cigars, the smell, the slimy tip, but it was such a business to smoke one he could generally do it without Cuthbert making him talk much. He slid down in the leather club chair and puffed away.

"I thought you were still in London," he said, to get Cuthbert talking.

TO MASTER THE TIDES

"I thought you knew your own house," said Cuthbert. "You're throwing a dinner party tonight, or had you forgot? I came to town for that. Your wife invited me and Lucy."

"I had forgotten, but it's no difference to me if there are others at dinner or not."

"Lord, Frederick. For Isabella's sake, I hope she's got something on the side."

Frederick only grimaced and puffed on his cigar.

"Speaking of on the side," continued Cuthbert, "Margery and Lord Fitton will be there tonight." Cuthbert waited for a reaction, but Frederick gave him none. "I am to assume you haven't taken back up with her?"

Frederick nodded. He hadn't.

"Good. I'm glad I gave you the shove then. She probably got something else right after you, anyway. Lots of young men in London who need an education in that way. You're not a man until you've had an intrigue and best to do it with someone with a reputation like that. One can't blame a young fool for a wanton with her legs open. No one blamed you. I made sure of it."

Frederick chewed on the end of the cigar. It was rather disgusting.

"You shouldn't talk of Margery that way," he said. "She has her good points even if she is a little touched. I don't regret her, whatever you may think."

"I'm not saying you should, only that you open your eyes about her. I hope you're not pining. Why, I even had the deuced woman."

"What?"

JOSEPHINE BORGIA

"Yes, back when you were still just a pup. Damned if I wasn't still a pup, too, only 16, but she was a good ride, I will tell you that. Lucy can't hold up."

Frederick spit out a sliver of tobacco that got into his mouth and stared at the burning end of the cigar. Why should that bother him? He and Margery had never said "no others." Frederick eyed his brother. His cheeks hadn't always been this puffy. Cuthbert had been decent enough to look at once upon a time, but Margery was so uptight in her tastes. It couldn't be the money, which was how Cuthbert was able to marry Lucy. Such thoughts left a sour taste in his mouth, more so even than the cigar.

Frederick smashed the butt of the cigar into the marble ash tray on the table, again and again, well after it was long out, oblivious to Cuthbert's horror at not putting it out correctly. "You roll it, man!" he said "What the devil is wrong with you!" Ignoring the advice, Frederick smashed the thing into oblivion, tobacco, and ashes spewing across the table. He nodded his apologies at a valet for the mess and left the club.

Frederick wasn't sure how he ended up on Margery's doorstep. The butler only raised an eyebrow and bade him wait. When the butler returned, Margery was home. Frederick had been in some doubt whether she would receive him. What was he doing here? What would he say to her when he saw her? The butler led him to the sitting room and sat him on a stuffed couch in front of the fire. Frederick rolled a cigarette and lit it in the blaze.

"Put that ghastly thing out," said Margery, sitting down on the chair across from him. "This room is mine. None of that filth in here."

TO MASTER THE TIDES

Frederick threw his cigarette into the fire, more than a little disappointed. He regarded Margery. She lounged on the sofa watching him just as close. It occurred to him he hadn't really looked at her since the night she threw him in the snow. She was a more subdued version of herself. She wore a low old lady's bun even though her hair was still dark. Her dress was dark, too, and flowed around her like a mantle. A few lines creased her cheeks, framing her mouth, but her eyes were still clear. They might even be clearer than they were the last time Frederick was with her. He couldn't be sure. It felt like so many years ago.

"What are you doing here, Frederick?" said Margery. "Don't tell me you want to take up again?"

"No. Not that."

"Is it your melancholy getting to you? Don't let Cuthbert be such a cunt about it. Shall I make you a drink? That always seems to lift it."

At his brother's name, Frederick's face soured. He remembered the puffy cheeks and the ridiculous mutton chops growing wilder every day. He replayed Cuthbert's words from this morning, *I've had her too*, over and over in his head. Why did it gall him so? He was happy to be free of Margery, but he looked at her again. She had aged well, and Cuthbert had not. Put them together and she was way above him. She was above Frederick as well. For the first time, he wondered why Margery chose to degrade herself with the likes of the Estibus men.

"I sat with Cuthbert today at the club," he said finally.

"Oh, Lord. Then I *will* get you a drink." Margery got up and poured him a finger of scotch. Frederick took it but only held it. Margery sat on the couch next to him. He could smell her jasmine, but it did not affect him as it used to. "What did he say that upset you? I'll still listen to you. I'll always listen to you."

"Why him?"

"Why him, what?"

"He said when he was younger, you and he ..."

"Oh, that? Frederick, that was so long ago. We were both different people. And he wasn't so repulsive to look at back then. You remember, he looked quite fine when he was young. You were scrawny. You both grew out, but you grew up to match it."

"Cuthbert is a horrible human. He always was."

"But I changed. I was more foolish back then and Cuthbert can be persuasive ..."

Margery didn't look at him when she said that; she only stared at the fire. Her face was unreadable. She noticed Frederick watching her and gave him a weary smile.

"Drink up. I'll join you." She made herself a drink and sat next to him. They didn't speak for a while, both staring at the fire, sinking deeper and deeper into the couch cushions.

Frederick never loved Margery. He saw that now but there was a comfort in her presence. The shows she put on, the vengeance she took, those were not her. At times, when she did not think he was watching, she appeared to him a trapped animal. He saw the same look when the hounds cornered the fox. Their conversations on the nights when he stayed until morning, there he got brief glimpses of her. How much did she know? She taught him more than he had ever learned at school, and there it was in that still dark head wasting away on dinner parties and fools like Isabella.

TO MASTER THE TIDES

Isabella was content in her world. Margery never had been. Frederick saw that now, clearer than day. He ought to apologize for throwing her over as he did. If he was an outlet for her, was she wrong to want to keep it? She sipped her drink but would not look at him.

"Do you believe in the Fae?" he asked finally.

"Yes," she said, still not looking at him. "Do you think you've seen one?"

"I do."

She turned to him with a hint of a smile. Her eyes searched his face, but she was not laughing at him.

"If you capture it," she said, "it will make you happy for a time. Take care to claim it properly or it will leave you."

That was the thing about her. She took him seriously when it mattered.

"I've lost her, already, I think."

"Tell me about her," said Margery, leaning her head back on the sofa and closing her eyes. Frederick complied, calling up all the details he could remember about the woman and the child. Then he told her about the night he first saw them, and the baby born in the moonlight. Even how he felt, holding the woman's hand.

"I very nearly did it that night, Margery. I had the pistol in my hand. The woman and her child saved me. They still do. Whenever *those* thoughts come, they remind me of that night, and her. I'm distracted and *those* thoughts don't come again."

"It sounds like you're already contracted to her." Margery took his hand and opened her eyes. "I'm glad. I'm glad she saved you. I know I couldn't anymore. There was a time when I was enough, but I'm not now. That's why you left. Not because of

JOSEPHINE BORGIA

Cuthbert or Isabella. If I was enough, what I was to you, you would have fought to stay. For all my years, I was still a child then, but I see it now. Lord, I still feel a child now. When do we finally feel like an adult, do you think? Does my hair have to gray? My tits sag?"

"I couldn't tell you."

Frederick squeezed her hand back, but it was not like the old days. No rush of passion. There were comfort and familiarity in her touch. He hadn't noticed when they started leaning arm to arm in front of the fire. They stayed there for some time.

"Why haven't you and Isabella had children?" Margery asked.

"My manhood froze off the night you threw me in the snow."

"Oh, bollox!" Margery laughed and swatted him.

"But really. There's something wrong with one of us or between us. It wasn't for lack of trying. We've given up on that now."

"I'm sorry for that."

"Likely for the best. Any children of ours would be miserable."

Margery sighed and watched him a moment but didn't speak. She downed the last of her drink and got up.

"I'm glad you came today," she said, "but you ought to be getting along. And Frederick ..."

Frederick got up and paused to hear what she would say. Her face was strained, more so than ever before.

TO MASTER THE TIDES

"Don't always take what Cuthbert says at face value. I'm sure you know your brother, but I've seen other sides of him, ones he doesn't show his family."

Frederick was curious but said nothing and took his leave.

Frederick passed Isabella on his way to the front door.

"What are you doing here?" she asked.

"Just a pop in," he said. "Wanted to ask Lady Fitton about Cuthbert."

"What about Cuthbert?" she asked, looking over his shoulder for Margery.

"Something he said to me today about when he was younger. He sounded full of hot air. I wanted to satisfy my curiosity."

"Oh, well, yes," she said, smiling wider than usual. "Your brother is quite full of it most of the time."

"Invite the Fittons to dinner tonight if you like," Frederick said. He was in the mood to be social for once. "We're not already entertaining, are we?"

"Only Cuthbert and Lucy."

"Cuthbert again," said Frederick with a sour expression. "Yes, do invite the Fittons. Might as well make a party of it. I can aim all Cuthy's conversation at Lord Fitton."

"Do you mean it?" asked Isabella. Frederick wondered that she behaved as if she hadn't already invited them. "What about the Whethertons? It's last-minute but I know they don't have plans this evening."

"Yes, yes, invite them, too. I promise to hold up my end of the conversation."

"Oh, Frederick, I'm not sure what's come over you, but I won't complain," she looked at him oddly a moment. "What did you do today? I cannot understand it. You make peace with my friend and now you want to have a party. Oh, don't look at me that way. Margery never said anything, but I had a sense that the two of you quarreled over something and someone was holding a grudge. I'm glad you've come round."

"I stopped at the coffee shop," Frederick said.

"We'll have to get the cook to learn to brew it, then." Isabella hesitated a moment and then grabbed Frederick's hand. "Thank you. I hope this is a new start for us. I know we have been at odds, but maybe we can be friends now?"

"I'll do my best."

Isabella took a deep breath and kissed him on the cheek. She did not look at him again as she hurried into the study.

The dining chandelier was near obscured from cigar smoke, but Frederick didn't mind it for once. He did not take a cigar himself, sticking to his cigarette. His head swam pleasantly with the after-dinner brandy and he laughed along with the other men, while they swore over politics. The ladies had adjourned to the drawing room. Frederick, Whetherton, Cuthbert, and Lord Fitton all sat around one end of the table.

"Frederick," said Cuthbert. "Don't know what's gotten into you tonight, man, but you're right jolly. I like this better than your usual doldrums."

Frederick said nothing but smiled and filled his brandy again.

"Margery was the same today," Fitton said. "I haven't seen her that animated in years, really. Not sure what it is."

Cuthbert eyed Frederick oddly but said nothing.

Seven

Frederick got out of bed early the next day despite a raging headache. He had gotten very drunk last night. Great God, what did he say to people? He didn't know. He hoped they didn't know, either. They all laughed a lot so that was something.

His feelings now ... the melancholy returned. Even more than that. Shame. Shame that dug a pit in his gut. It was the alcohol and his disposition. They didn't mix. What happened to that feeling of wellbeing he had yesterday? It was in the sweet shop, behind the veil. He wanted it back, but that would require getting up. What time was it even? The valet bustled into the room and found Frederick lying in bed and staring at the ceiling.

"Do you wish to rise and dress today, Sir?" asked the valet, pausing before the closet door.

Frederick said nothing and rolled out of bed.

It was well past mid-day. The guests milled about the house. Frederick did not take the time to find any of them. Isabella would likely be more content without him. Once he was sure he was fit to be seen and did not look like he had two black eyes, he headed out and called for the carriage.

In town, it was pleasant that day. The sun was out, and the warmth of spring mixed in with the lingering winter chills.

JOSEPHINE BORGIA

Frederick retraced his steps. First, he went to the club. The book he left sat untouched on a side table. No one appreciated the stoics anymore. He went by the sweet shop but was obliged to sit at the counter as all the tables were full. He sipped his coffee and ignored everyone. This wasn't the same. He couldn't see out the windows without twisting around. The veil was gone. There was no peace here.

Frederick finished his cuppa and headed out, deciding which way to go. He peeped in the milliners but there were no customers. He wandered aimlessly down the street until he came to the park. It was as good a place to wander aimlessly, and he wondered how much time he could waste there before he grew tired and hungry.

After a bit, he sat on a bench. The sun beat down now, and he had a raging headache. If the guests stayed on, he would be in for it again tonight. That might not be so bad. His head hurt but his stomach was strong. He ought to go back. Have a quick afternoon pull and a nap until it was time to dress for dinner. Instead, he remained on the bench, just as he remained in bed that morning.

Frederick watched the people go by, gazing at each face, guessing their thoughts. Did melancholy weigh on any of them like it did him or were they obliviously happy? He looked for something among the crowd. Not the Fae woman and the Fairy child. They were long gone. But a secret. That's what he looked for. He followed the smiling faces and the laughing conversation. People were smiling and laughing *sober*. What was their secret? What was it? Why did he care? It didn't matter, anyway. It didn't matter a jot what he did to anyone.

TO MASTER THE TIDES

But still. He had a moment of happiness yesterday. It was in the sweet shop, no when he saw the girl and the woman. What he did mattered. They were alive because he was there. Something he did mattered, after all. He wanted to see them again. He needed to know they were happy.

That night the guests stayed onto the next. It rained a good deal and the road down the hill was nigh on impassible. Frederick drank and feigned happiness. Isabella was overjoyed to have company. She seemed happier than she had been in years. Everyone did. Still, Frederick, could not help but anticipate the clouds rolling in. He wanted to talk about it, such an unmanly thing to do, but he did.

It was early morning. Everyone had gone to bed only an hour ago. Frederick's head spun but he couldn't sleep. The same thoughts churned over and over in his head. *I want to see her. I want to know she's well. Perhaps I can do something for the little fairy girl. They saved me. I owe it to them.*

Frederick got out of bed though he didn't exactly know why. He poured a glass of water from the ewer and drank it down. After splashing more water on his face, he tried to focus on his reflection in the mirror. It was dark and there was not much to see. Only one eye shone in the dim blue light. *Where is the rest of me?* He snickered. *I'm too in my cups still. I want to talk. I want to talk all about it.* Frederick stumbled into the hall.

He wondered where the other guests had lodged. Four neat rooms, all in a row. None of the couples stayed together. What a joke that was. You were supposed to save yourself for one and no other but the window for that ended so quickly unless you were a brute, which he was not. And brutes from what he could understand didn't generally save themselves, either. Ridiculous.

JOSEPHINE BORGIA

Frederick stopped short and swayed in the hall. Someone was coming. Their footsteps were light.

"Isabella," he muttered.

The shadow of a person stopped.

"Frederick?" It *was* Isabella. "Frederick, what are you doing up?" she said in a rush. "You weren't coming to see me, were you? You know, we've had such a pleasant few days."

Frederick tried to focus on her with one eye half-closed. He was vaguely conscious of how much he swayed while he stood there. Isabella seemed a little panicky. Poor woman. Was she afraid of him? He didn't want her to be. He shook his head.

"Not that. Drunk. Got the spins. Couldn't lie down. What are you doing up?"

"My room is so stuffy. I wanted to peek out on the terrace for a bit, get some air."

"The stairs are back that way."

"So they are. Still drunk, too!"

Frederick laughed and clapped her on the shoulder like an old school chum. She turned and went back down the hall to the stairs. He stood where he was and watched her until she was gone before he remembered where he was going.

Margery groaned when she opened her door.

"You can't be serious, Frederick," she said. "I know we've been having a time these last few days..."

"I don't want a roll," Frederick said. "I just want to talk. Not about us even. Just talk."

She rolled her eyes and let him in. "Fine, lie down," she said, lighting a candle on her side table. "Try not to lose your stomach on the bedding. I'd have to take the blame and my reputation would be shot. I've never vomited anywhere that wasn't proper. I've always made it to the basin or the garden and none saw me do it."

Frederick flopped down on the bed, face first in a pillow, and Margery pulled up a chair.

"Are you sure you're well enough to talk?"

Frederick nodded.

"Go on then if you can. Do you want another drink? You do leave good scotch for your guests, after all."

"Remnant from my uncle."

"Good man, he was. Now talk. That's what you came for, isn't it?"

"I want to see her, them, but I don't know how."

"Who?"

"The Fae and the Fairy. It's the only time I've ever been happy, Margery. Can you understand?"

Margery got up and poured herself a scotch. She took a long drink before she sat back down again. She brushed Frederick's curly hair back from his forehead.

"Can you not see them?"

"I think I have to be behind the veil."

Margery sighed again and leaned back. "I see. Now you make no sense. Just talk. I'm going to drink my scotch and listen. If I fall asleep in the chair, pay no mind."

Frederick watched her but didn't talk. The light in the room grew. Margery watched him too. He traced the lines of her face and the long slender fingers holding the glass as she raised it to her lips. She had aged but she was there, underneath it all. How in love he fancied himself when they first met. He thought of the first time he saw her, already married but still flush with life in the Bath assembly room. Back then, dresses were fuller, and women wore chignons to puff out their hair.

People danced, though intentionally not with each other. She always seemed to be lined up next to him, her hand in his whenever they were to dance with their neighbors. How foolish he was then not to see that was by design. He still did like the curves of her face.

"What is it?" Margery said. Her smile had a hint of shyness. Frederick took her hand and placed it on his manhood. Margery laughed at him.

"Lord, Frederick," she said. "Do you remember nothing? That only puts me off. You have to kiss my neck or run your thumb along my chin. You might have had a chance had you tried to seduce me. I was remembering old times while we sat here, but if you won't talk, and you're going to be a clod about it, I have no use for you. Get out before the maid comes to wake me. I don't need talk if I haven't even had the fun to earn it."

Frederick grumbled but got up. The room had stopped spinning and his eyes were closing on their own even as he walked. Margery succeeded in him out the door and bolted it after him. Was that necessary?

Back in his room, he fell across the bed lengthwise. The sun was coming up in earnest now, but he drifted off anyway. Bright green eyes haunted his fitful dreams.

It was near two weeks before the guests could leave. Isabella went with Margery for a good long visit and Frederick was alone. The first day after she left, he went to the park again and sat on a bench near the fountain to watch the faces. It was warm now and the splash from the fountain cool on his face. A few trees flowered. They smelled sweet but made his eyes water.

TO MASTER THE TIDES

Frederick sneezed a few times and wiped his eyes to get them out of the fog. That was when he saw them. They were across the plaza on the other side of the fountain.

The fairy looked right at him, piercing him with her green eyes. The Fae didn't see him, but Frederick finally got a look at her. Her hair was black as coal tied tight. She wore a tweed lady's suit, the full skirt a few years out of fashion. The jacket was buttoned up to her chin. She seemed to be trying to contain herself. Today she was moving fast, dragging the little one behind her. The fairy stopped for a moment when she shared at Frederick. The Fae tugged her hand, perhaps a little too hard, and scolded her to hurry. The little girl trotted along after her, but she had dropped something.

Frederick jumped to his feet and called after them. The thing got kicked about by the passing people. Frederick pushed his way through the crowd and snatched up the thing. It was a tiny stuffed bear. The arms, legs, and head moved. The poor bear looks dirty and sad. Frederick shoved it in his pocket and looked around for the Fairy and the Fae. Again, they were gone.

Frederick went home after that. He asked for a basin of water and a scrub brush. He sat on the terrace with it, sleeves rolled up like a regular working man, and scrubbed the bear clean. He fancied it was happier now.

At dinner that night, his shirt cuffs and collar chaffed something awful. Isabella was still at the Fittons, so he had no one to complain to. The sun burnt his skin out on the terrace. The clean little bear sat on the table next to his wine glass. The servants said nothing but were careful not to knock it over.

He would not complain to the bear, not when it seemed so content.

The next day Frederick retraced his steps in town, again and again, walking in circles to the places where he saw them before. He asked at shops. Most hadn't seen them. The sales lady at the milliner seemed wary when he asked.

"What do you want with the lady?"

"She dropped something the other day, and I would like to give it back."

"She's got an order in with us. Give it to me and I'll hand it to her."

Frederick clutched the little bear in his jacket pocket.

"You see, it's..." He paused a moment. That wouldn't do. "It's of a personal nature. I would rather hand it to her myself. You understand?"

The woman nodded but narrowed her eyes.

"Will she be in soon for her order, you think?" he asked.

"Nay. She said she won't be in for another month. Off visiting a relative, down by the sea."

Isabella was home that evening and brought the Fittons. Frederick was thankful Cuthbert and Lucy weren't with them. Dinner was subdued. He left the bear upstairs on his night table. Margery had her eyes on him all through the meal. Frederick sipped his wine faster than he likely should have.

Frederick went to bed early while the others sat up. He didn't sleep, only let his candle burn, and stared at the little bear on the night table. He thought too much about it. That was certain, but the bear let him remember the Fae and the Fairy. He blew out the candle and laid back on his pillow but still could not sleep.

TO MASTER THE TIDES

He should not have been surprised at the knock on his door. Margery came in and closed the door behind her before he could answer the knock. She was in her nightdress. They didn't talk. Before, she would give him abuse or plead with him, depending on her mood. This time, she only waited by the door. Frederick went to her and rubbed his thumb down the side of her chin. He gathered her into his arms—why did she feel so fragile? Why did he feel so old? He kissed her. It wasn't a rush of passion, but it was familiar, safe. Her arms crept around his neck and he pulled down the collar of her nightdress to kiss her shoulder.

"What is that?" she asked, pointing at the bear on his nightstand.

"It doesn't matter," he said continuing up her neck.

The next morning, Margery was gone, and the bear was in the waste can. Frederick rescued it and stowed it in his writing desk.

Frederick continued his aimless wandering in town with the stuffed creature safe in his pocket. He would not let it out of his sight again. The Fae and the Fairy wouldn't be in town, but he wanted to tread where they tread. He was drawn to their path like a humble dog following his pack. He sipped coffee at the high table and ignored the ladies whispering in the room. He went to the club and napped in the stuffed chairs and dreamed of grass-green eyes.

This is all too much. I have to dispose of this thing. Frederick left the club and headed back toward the milliner. He should wrap the bear and give it to the shop lady to deliver. He had made such a to-do about it being personal; now, it was embarrassing. He could ask for her address and send it to her,

JOSEPHINE BORGIA

but it wasn't likely the shopkeeper would give it out. He could lay himself out, say he felt foolish before, but he really did want the girl to have her bear. Frederick paced in front of the store, talking himself through what he wanted to say. He reached in his pocket and paused when he touched the velveteen fur.

"May I help you, sir?" The sales lady peeked her head out of the shop, keeping the door between her and Frederick.

"Possibly, er, well, no, never mind." Frederick turned on his heel and strode off toward the park, his face beet red. *God help me if I need a hat soon.*

Back at home, he kept the little bear in a pigeonhole of the writing desk in his room. Locking the desk gave him an odd satisfaction that the toy was safe. He didn't want Margery to see it again. It might get tossed. *All this over a toy.* He shook his head at himself and tried to forget about the bear and the Fae and the Fairy while he dressed for dinner.

At dinner, he bolted down his drinks, even though his stomach still roiled from this week's excess. Isabella had Cuthbert and Lucy again. Frederick stayed quiet while the other three talked. There was no need to listen, only nod and agree when his brother demanded his attention. They never asked him any questions. Rather, they had given up on asking him questions. He did little with his day and none of them were interested in the books he read.

The talk droned on around Frederick, but it was all noise to him. He had the servant bring him some brandy with his dessert. He swirled it around in the snifter and watched it make perfect rings around the glass, little tides of his own making. What did he want, really? Not this. Not conversation that meant nothing. A marriage that meant nothing. He was tired of simply passing the time until it was over. If he survived that night at the gamekeeper's cabin, ought it not to be for something?

"Well, what do you think? Good idea, no?" Cuthbert asked.

"What? Well, yes. Capital idea."

"Do you mean it?" asked Isabella, glowing.

"Yes, well, yes I do." *Bollox, what did I agree to?*

"Frederick!" she said, coming round the table and kissing him on the cheek. "I'm glad. Come!" she said to Isabella. "Let's make all the plans before the men come to the drawing room." Two went off, heads down, whispering all the way.

Cuthbert laughed a little too hard while he lit his cigar and choked on the smoke. He still snickered after he got control of his hacking fit.

"Did that on purpose, you know," he said, winking at Frederick. "I know you don't listen to a damned thing. Like talking to a wall. I was lucky I got a response out of you a 'tall. You can't back out now that your wife is so happy, so don't even think it."

"What am I not to back out of?" There was no point in trying to pretend he knew.

"The lot of us are going for a stay with the Fittons at their house in Brighton next week. It's maybe too cold for sea bathing but still a pleasant spot in the spring."

Frederick massaged his temples with one hand. It was true—he couldn't get out of it. Whatever she thought, he did care if Isabella was happy or not and would do what he could to make her so. It was the least he could do in their situation.

"I'll soldier through, I suppose," he said, lighting a cigarette.

JOSEPHINE BORGIA

"At least try to have fun while you're there. Or perhaps not," Cuthbert eyed Frederick. "You haven't taken back up with Margery, have you?"

"Just the once."

"The deuce, Frederick. What did I tell you? If you want to get rid of them, you have to stop fucking them. Doesn't matter. This will make for a more interesting trip than I imagined."

Eight

Brighton was gentle during the day but still chilly at night. The Fittons and both pairs of Estibuses huddled together as they hurried down the sidewalk, the wind off the ocean biting their cheeks. Frederick felt they could have waited to see the play, but Cuthbert was adamant they go. There were two playhouses in town. The Ormerod was the more respectable one but the Dalton had better players. Frederick wasn't sure which they were going to tonight. He trudged along with the rest keeping his hat pulled tight over his ears.

Isabella clung tight to his arm out of chill rather than affection, but Frederick didn't mind the warm body close to him. Had it been proper, he would have pulled Margery in on the other side. She didn't seem to notice the cold. She walked straight and tall, long white neck exposed to the air as if it was a pleasant summer day. Cuthbert led the way, letting Lucy huff to keep pace behind him. Lord Fitton hung back and puffed on his pipe.

"Here," said Cuthbert, stopping at a cross street. "Let's cross here. More people over there. It'll be much warmer." The group followed his lead and melted into the crowd.

"Where did you say we were going?" Frederick asked, but a gust blew just then, and Cuthbert's answer was lost on the wind. The group trudged on. Isabella let go of his arm and hugged herself, teeth chattering. Frederick offered her his coat, but she waved him off. That made him sour. He wasn't trying anything. He knew she didn't care for him that way anymore but was it so terrible of him to do a kind thing?

Frederick kept walking, watching his shoe tips and the hem of Lucy's dress in front of him. Why had he come? Well, why not? There was nothing to do at home. There was nothing of interest to him here either, so really it was no matter what he did. It was easier to get pushed around by the tide of your peers' wants than want anything yourself. Even if he did claim something he wanted, the tide would take it back out again. What was the point? His feet were sore already and he wanted a smoke. He was going to ask how much farther, but when he looked around him, he was alone.

People were everywhere, just not his people. They skirted around him and did not look his way as if he were not there. He stood on tiptoe, trying to see above the crowd. Lord Fitton was likely the only one he might spot. He sighed and pulled out a smoke, turning here and there to shield it from the wind while he lit it. Succeeding, he took a long drag and blew the smoke up into the air obscuring his vision. He turned to walk back in the direction he was headed before and bumped a woman. She teetered for a moment, but Frederick caught her by the arm and kept her on her feet.

"Terribly sorry. I..." His voice caught in his throat as he stared down at the heart-shaped face. Bundled in a great plaid cloak, it was her, the Fae. He still had her arm in his hand. It felt so fragile, so thin, he hoped he hadn't hurt her. She stared back up at him, her face quite pretty when not strained in childbirth. And her eyes. He remembered her eyes from that night and even out in the middle of the street, they stared through you. She could outwit him on everything. He saw all of that there. Not like Margery, who taught like an old nun with a ruler. This woman was cleverer than them all.

"No trouble. Thank you." The woman extracted herself from his grip and trotted off into the crowd.

Frederick went after her. People noticed him now. He bumped and jostled and shoved, not caring who he might vex. Where was she? He couldn't see her among the crowd of people, she was so small. He kept an eye out for any bit of plaid that might show through an opening, but he saw none. On he went until he was off the main strip and the crowd had thinned to almost nothing. She was nowhere. No, that wasn't true. She was here. Here in Brighton. He could ask around about her. What family did she belong to? She wouldn't be in their circle. Not wandering about with her husband the way they were. By the feel of her arm, she didn't eat much. What had happened to her husband? Frederick hadn't seen him any of the times he saw the woman and the girl. If the man was a layabout, Frederick might have words with him. Or not. He had no claim.

Frederick took another cigarette out of the case but a grab at his arm fouled up his attempt to light it. He turned, a great grin on his face, expecting to see a plaid cloak and heart-shaped face, but it was Lucy.

"Thank goodness I found you," she said. "I don't know where anyone has got off to."

"You were separated, too?" He put away his cigarette; Lucy had spoiled his last match. "I thought I was the only fool who got lost."

"No. I did as well. I was going along, trying to keep up with Cuthy and suddenly he was gone. No one else was there either. What were you doing?"

"Looking." He didn't say for who.

"Well, we'll have to keep looking."

"Did Cuthbert not tell you which theater we were going to?"

"I could have sworn the Ormerod, but I went by and no one else was there. Do you think they went in without us?"

"I doubt that. We'll give the Dalton a try. Maybe he doesn't have straight which is which."

Frederick let Lucy huddle close. It was too chilly to worry about being proper at this point. Frederick cursed Brighton in the spring. Spring was supposed to be warm and pleasant, not a winter that crept into your bones.

They went by the Dalton, but no one was there, either. Up and down the streets they walked, pausing under the gas lights to stand on tiptoe to survey the crowds. All the while, Lucy looked for their company and Frederick for a plaid cloak.

After a half-hour of searching, they decided to try the Ormerod again. It was too late to see the show, but the others might wait for them there. Or perhaps they might as well go home and drink away the night's failure. It was worrisome, however, that no one was turning up. Frederick had never heard of muggers in Brighton, but one never knew.

At the Ormerod, the Fittons stood out front. Both waved like maniacs when they spotted Lucy and Frederick. The four of them huddled together for warmth and Lord Fitton pulled out a flask and passed it around.

TO MASTER THE TIDES

"So, what the deuce do we do now?" said Lord Fitton, pulling out a second flask. He sounded as if he had downed the first. "Estibus is such a fool about those things. Never knows where he was going."

Margery took the second flask from him and took a drink but didn't say anything.

"Try the Dalton again?" suggested Frederick.

"Tried that," said Fitton. "Not there."

"He's not here, either," said Lucy, taking her turn with the alcohol. She drank seldom and after two or three pulls, her eyes were already swimming.

"We can't keep walking back and forth all night," Frederick said. "We ought to get a carriage and go home."

"Yes, perhaps," Margery said. "Isabella might be alone out here, though. We aren't sure she found Cuthbert. Did you forget her, Frederick?"

"No," said Frederick, taking the flask back from Lucy. He had.

The group took a roundabout way back to the Dalton to look down as many side streets as they could. The crowds were thinning now, and it was easier to look and not get lost but Cuthbert and Isabella didn't turn up. They paused at the Dalton entrance, passing round the flasks, while music and laughter trickled out from inside the theater.

"I am a little sorry we didn't get to see a show tonight," said Lucy. "I was looking forward to it." Her face hung and she toed a buckled stone in the pavement over and over.

Frederick felt for her. He didn't care where he was, but Lucy so rarely got entertainment away from the children. This was to be a trip for her enjoyment in particular. Damn

JOSEPHINE BORGIA

Cuthbert for flying through the crowd like that. Lucy had a small stride. How the deuce did he expect her to keep up?

"There you are, you blasted wretches!" Cuthbert and Isabella were there at last.

"Lucy!" said Cuthbert, red in the face. His brows were screwed up in a bushy line. "How many times must I remind you not to get lost?"

"Now, Cuthy," she said, shrinking. Her eyes welled up. "I didn't. I promise. I went straight to the Ormerod as soon as I realized I was separated from everyone."

"And you had to take the whole lot around with you!"

"Really, Cuthbert," said Frederick, taking his brother's arm. It was best to diffuse Cuthbert early. "We all got lost."

Cuthbert knocked Frederick away. Lucy covered her face with a handkerchief.

"Don't muddle things. I told her the Dalton and she knows it."

"I swear I heard the Ormerod."

"What were you doing all night? We waited and waited."

"I tried the Dalton too, but..."

"You didn't stay put and now we've been wandering back and forth all night?!"

"Cuthbert," said Margery, handing him one of the flasks. "Take a drink and don't be a shite."

Cuthbert threw the flask on the ground and cursed Margery. He turned back to Lucy, but Frederick had already ushered Isabella and Lucy down the street. The Fittons were behind them. Cuthbert yelled after them. They stopped a cabbie carriage and left Cuthbert to fend for himself.

TO MASTER THE TIDES

The week went by. The group never did make it to the theater. Lucy and Cuthbert behaved as if nothing happened, but the party spirit of the trip was subdued. Lord Fitton returned to the country a few days after the theater incident. The ladies spent time together, ignoring the men. Cuthbert spent his time in card halls while Frederick laid in his room most of the day. He took frequent naps and said little at mealtimes, all the while thinking of the woman he saw. There had to be some reason she kept crossing his path. Perhaps the same few people always cross your path every day, but until you recognize them, you never notice. This woman was merely familiar.

Frederick dressed, not bothering to ring for a servant, and went downstairs. He found the ladies in the sitting room. Conversation hushed as soon as he came in.

"Don't let me stop you," said Frederick, going to the liquor cabinet and pouring himself some scotch and taking a chair by the fire.

"We were speaking of woman troubles," said Margery. "I'm sure you wouldn't want to hear the details."

Frederick got up and went to the library.

The others milled about the house and Cuthbert was nowhere to be found. At the end of the evening, it was only Margery and Frederick still up in the drawing room, sitting in front of the fire. They were both well lubricated with brandy. Frederick felt far from warm. Without the lively conversation to direct his thoughts, he turned inward on himself, rehashing every tiny thing he did not like. Now, he watched the log on the hearth burn away, the edges crumbling to ash, bit by bit.

"Something about me has to change," he said. Margery sipped her brandy a moment.

"You have changed," she said. "Look at yourself, on a trip, surrounded by friends."

"Outwardly maybe, I have, but that's only a shell. The shell is thickening and squeezing out what's left inside. Maybe all that is inside is the melancholy and attempts at intellectualism, but I want to keep it. I want to keep the meat of myself intact and not have it pushed about by this hardened shell. Something must change. Everything must change. Can you understand that?"

"What are you getting at, Frederick? We all want to be better people but what is the point? Don't tell me you've got religious all of a sudden."

"It isn't even about that. But I can't take back up with you."

"Not this again. You always come back."

Margery didn't look at him. She took up a poker and shoved the logs around in the hearth. The fire stoked up hot. The heat burned on Frederick's cheeks even sitting as far back as he was.

"I won't this time. I can't. I can go on doing all the things I've always done or else I will be eaten alive."

"By me?" Margery raised an eyebrow.

"Yes, and everything else along with you."

"What will you do? Run away? Leave your poor little wife in that nasty house on the hill? Will you leave your brother?"

"Yes," said Frederick, crossing his arms against his chest. "Damn them all."

"Do you mean it? Damn me even?"

"Yes, to a point."

TO MASTER THE TIDES

Margery pulled the poker out of the fire and held up the tip. The end looked as it always did, the same, untouched by the tiny hearth blaze, but it was burning hot. *It's like Margery in a way,* Frederick mused. *Looks just like it always does, but in truth is dangerous.*

"You know what I was just thinking," said Frederick with a cynical laugh. "That poker..."

Margery brought down the hot end of the poker on the back of Frederick's hand. Bits of his flesh seared to it when she pulled it back. Margery smiled as she examined the point of the poker. She shoved it back in the fire to burn off the skin.

"Don't ever think you can get away from me, Frederick," she said. "I know you fancy yourself contracted off somewhere else, but what if you had a similar contract with me? Did you not understand the terms of the bargain you made?"

Margery finally looked at him. Her face was calm but her eyes wild.

Frederick backed away from her, nursing his hand that bled from where the skin ripped. He pulled out a handkerchief and wrapped it up. Margery watched, eying the blood soaking through the wrap with only a hint of a grin. Neither of them spoke. Frederick got up and backed out of the room.

Frederick didn't care where he went. It was night but the moon was full. It was much like the moon the night he went to the gamekeeper's cabin, but he would not let himself think about that. He walked out the back of the house, through the garden. He found a door in the fence and went through. Once out he paused. The sand and sea, the full moon just above, expanding on forever before him. A tang of salt and fish was in the air and something else. There was a whiff of morning glories.

The wild night surf called to Frederick, and he pushed through the grasses that grew near the ocean and out into the sand. He took a long breath of the sea air. It was warmer tonight and didn't burn his lungs. Gazing out over the water, he imagined what it would be like to soar up above it, on and on forever. He gazed up and down the beach, deciding if he should take a walk or kick off his shoes and brave the water.

There she was. Frederick had missed her in the dark, but now his eyes adjusted, or else she materialized out of nowhere. She stood on the beach, perhaps 100 feet away, but there was no mistaking the plaid cloak or heart-shaped white face that challenged the moon with its brightness, Frederick walked toward her, drawn as if he were caught in a spell. *Don't move. Don't go. Wait for me. Please wait for me.*

She did. The woman saw him but waited. Frederick took a minute to catch his breath before he could speak to her. She waited expectantly.

"Do you remember me?" he asked.

"Yes, how could one forget an experience like what we shared?"

"Oh, good. I was worried you would run from me. You know, a strange gent in the middle of the night."

She shook her head. "I recognized you the second I saw you, otherwise I would have. I saw you before you saw me, though I wasn't sure you would want to talk to me."

"I do want to talk to you. I have something of yours, not here with me, but it's at the house where I'm staying."

TO MASTER THE TIDES

"Oh? Did I drop something when I saw you in town last week?"

"Um, no." Frederick messed with his hair, feeling foolish. Only then did he notice he had gone out without a hat. "It was your girl who dropped it, back in the park."

"You found Zeus!" she said, delighted. "Abby will be so pleased."

"You did name her Abigail?!"

"I did."

"Would you like to walk a bit? I feel so foolish. I don't know anything about you."

The woman's name was Ellie Miller. Her husband died in a drunken brawl soon after their daughter was born. She wasn't sorry to lose him, though things were difficult for a time. Her father passed on only a year after that. He wasn't much better than the husband, but he was a merchant and left her a bit of money. Things were never quite as well as one wished but they got on. She was in Brighton visiting a cousin.

"It is good to have family around," Ellie said. "I worry Abby is too isolated with me. And I'm selfish, I know, but in Brighton, I get to be alone here and there. Don't you feel it, with the ocean and sky going on forever? How very alone we are? It makes one free."

Frederick hadn't thought about it but now he felt what she meant. With him, though, it left a hole in his chest down to his gut. His whole life he was always alone, deep within himself.

"I'm sorry," Ellie said. "Forgive me. My mother always said my head was amongst the clover."

"It's not what you said, only, no, never mind." He mussed his hair again.

JOSEPHINE BORGIA

"God's bollox! What happened to your hand?"

"Oh, that." Frederick had completely forgotten about his injury. The handkerchief was nearly soaked through with blood. "Tripped. Run in with fireplace."

Ellie grabbed his hand and peeled back the bandage with care. Frederick noted the cold little points of her fingertips against his palm. His hand seemed ungainly and rough in comparison. And still, she crushed his fingers the time he held that hand.

"We need to attend to this," she said. "How are you taking with a straight face? I'm sure this hurts."

Frederick shrugged.

"Come with me to my cousins."

"I couldn't. That wouldn't be proper."

"I suppose not. Of course, you're a gentleman, after all. But come. I can't leave you like this if you won't care for yourself."

Ellie pinched the back of Frederick's arm, just as his nanny used to, and dragged him to a nearby water pump. As she cleaned the wound, it smarted again, but he held still, if only to feel the Fae fingers on the back of his hand. That's what they were, Fae fingers. Nearly translucent in the moonlight.

Ellie tore a strip off her petticoat and tsked when Frederick objected. She wrapped his hand tightly and watched it a moment to make sure it didn't bleed through. Frederick flexed his hand and found it felt a little better.

"May I call on you tomorrow?" Frederick asked. "I'd like to return Zeus."

"You have him here? I'm sorry, but I promised Abby we would see the ocean tomorrow. We leave in two days and I'm afraid we might not get another chance, the weather being so fickle."

"I can bring him to you here," said Frederick. "Don't worry. I won't interrupt your day. I'll drop off the bear and go."

"Very well, Mr. Estibus, was it?" said Ellie, smiling—how odd it was that was the first time he saw that. It was like the sun coming out in the middle of the night. "I will look for you tomorrow."

Nine

Frederick escaped in the early morning. Not that he thought she would be there yet. He knew she wouldn't. He didn't want to see Margery at breakfast. He didn't want her to see the new bandages and that someone else had repaired what she tried to destroy. He couldn't stay in her house any longer. His waking hours would be best spent wandering.

The kitchen staff stopped what they were doing when he sneaked through and grabbed a piece of toast. He held his finger to his lips, winking at each one. He didn't have much hope they wouldn't tattle on him, but he didn't care. Through the garden he went. The statues at the Fittons were much like the ones his father had in London. He stopped at the one of Poseidon. This version showed the god sweeping his trident through the air. The early morning mist hung all around the base, just right for hiding fairies and brownies. An odd mix of mythology but Frederick still felt their presence. It was thick in the muted hush of the foggy morning.

Down on the beach, waves crashed hard onto the shore. The ocean was rough, angry. It would not be a good day to challenge it. Great steel blue waves rose up and down, churning up the hapless fish and seaweed, tossing them to shore and dragging them out again. The sky was cloudy and bleak, numb to the torment of the small creatures below. The rise of the

TO MASTER THE TIDES

waves made Frederick uneasy. He clutched the little bear tight in his pocket and considered turning back, but no. Not today. He would brave Poseidon today. Zeus would protect him.

Frederick wandered alone for some time. The air was a bit chill, but he didn't notice it. He was determined to do battle with the sea until he saw Ellie again. What was it about her that held his thoughts so completely? The circumstances under which they met, surely. Still, he would have found her compelling had they met under the most ordinary of chances. What did she think about the world? Did she read? Did she pray? He had so many questions he felt they could never answer. She met the world head-on, he knew that. She survived on her own with her daughter, even before she came into some money. He would be lost if he were all alone, without his uncle's money.

The thought struck him that he had never really taken care of himself. Servants dressed him, prepared his food, woke him. Tenants worked his land, and he did nothing all day but mope about. He did no work. He made nothing. He would leave no legacy when he died. It was a damning feeling. He sat in the sand, only a little back from where the waves reached, feeling the sting of the spray on his face. He pulled Zeus out of his pocket and set him on his knee.

"I'm sorry you're stuck with such a foolish man," Frederick said. "You'll be back home soon. I would say it is time for me to get home too but I don't know that I belong anywhere. I go where I am pushed. I'm a child, really." The spray kicked up high and he put the bear back in his pocket.

The sun came out late morning. Frederick took off his jacket and hat. He'd long taken off his shoes and stockings and rolled up his pants. He ought to have brought some food with him, or a flask, but it wouldn't do to meet the woman and child drunk.

There she was again, as if out of thin air. She was far away still. Ellie seemed to float down the beach in her blue, spring dress. The skirt was full in the old fashion, gauzy and ethereal. Abby skipped in circles about her mother, blond hair shining in the sun. Ellie carried a basket, blanket, and a great umbrella and was dwarfed by her cargo. Frederick hurried forward to them.

Ellie smiled when he reached them. She was huffing and red in the face with her burden. Frederick took the umbrella and blanket from her and let her breathe a bit.

"I'm glad to see you," she said, catching her breath.

"I'm good for manpower, at least," he said. "Forgive my disarray. It gets hot out."

"You look like a hobo," Ellie said with a wry smile, "but come sit with us a moment. It wouldn't do for you to get heat exhaustion."

Frederick complied and helped Ellie spread the blanket and put up the umbrella. He hadn't noticed how much the sun had gotten to him until he took a seat in the shade. His eyes were spotty.

"Lie down, if you need to," said Ellie, pulling a canteen out of the basket and handing it to him. "Abby, come here. You must put on your bonnet. I let you leave it off on the way here, but the sun is too hot, and you'll burn."

The child pouted but did as she was told. She sat down on the blanket as well and eyed Frederick while her mother tied the bonnet ribbons under her chin.

"You found Zeus!" she said.

TO MASTER THE TIDES

"I did," said Frederick. He fished around in his jacket pocket and pulled out the little bear. The girl snatched him back and giggled, whispering to the bear.

"He says you were kind to him," Abby said. "Not everyone is kind to him."

"I tried to be. He deserved rescuing. I'm glad he is back to you."

She turned the bear's leg so that he was in a sitting position on the blanket.

"I'm going to play now. Mama, will you watch him?"

"Yes, of course, darling. Stay close. Don't go out into the water."

Frederick got up to take his leave, but Abby grabbed his sleeve.

"Zeus says he wants you to watch him, too."

Frederick sat back down.

"Very well, just for a little."

The two of them watched Abby play in the sand, pulling up sticks and making paths for the waves to run into. She never seemed to tire. Ellie made Frederick eat one of the sandwiches she brought. "My cousin's kitchen lady always makes too much," she said. Frederick ate and felt better than he had in a long time. Ellie also brought a strip of linen and some ointment for his hand. She scolded him dreadfully for not changing it out when he got home. The last bandage was fine for an emergency but was awfully dirty. Frederick took his scolding in good grace but even Ellie's Fae fingers were not gentle when she ripped off the old bandage. That done, they sat quiet again.

JOSEPHINE BORGIA

"I'm glad we met again," she said, after a time. "I never thanked you properly for what you did. Abby and I might not have survived otherwise."

"I'm glad I'm of use to someone," Frederick said.

"You are of great use, I'm sure."

"My family doesn't think so. They tolerate me."

"Why not go your own way? Things are not like they used to be. Even women have options now. When my first husband died, I thought for sure I would have to wed again to survive. Now, even if the money runs out, I could find work. I would need to learn to type or something like that, but I could take care of us."

"I can't type," said Frederick, smiling. "It doesn't matter. My fate is so inextricably tied to the tides and whims of my family, I have no choice in anything."

"Surely you don't have a care?"

"Is that what you think? I was thinking about just that myself before you arrived. I thought about how I do nothing in this world but take up space."

"What would you do if you could do anything?" asked Ellie.

"I don't know. I don't know what I want." Frederick paused and took a deep breath. Ellie waited for him to speak, eyes expectant. She seemed so young, but her cares had drawn lines on her face and under her eyes. She understood. She would understand. "There is a dream I always have," he began. "It seems like it's nothing, but I feel like it has to do with everything. It is everything. I am lying on the beach and the tides come in. I never get up. I always lie there letting the water come in around me. Sometimes it is cold and sometimes it is warm, but I always float, nose barely above the surface. It is stifling even when it is comfortable. I wish I could swim, or stop the tide altogether, like Poseidon, but I can do nothing except keep breathing while the water pushes me about."

"You want to be a master of the tides," Ellie said. It wasn't a question. "You want control of your own life."

Frederick didn't answer.

"What about you?" he asked. "What do you want?"

Ellie smiled to herself a moment.

"For Abby to grow up healthy and happy," she said. "I know that's no answer. It's not that I don't want to tell you, only that I don't think you'll believe me."

"You don't have to," Frederick said, "but you may, if you wish."

"Perhaps I will," said Ellie. "Will you tell me what really happened to your hand? Is someone cruel to you?"

Frederick wasn't sure how to answer this. She shouldn't be concerned for him. He was a man, after all. He could defend himself against Margery. Even as the thought crossed his mind, he felt foolish. There was no defense against Margery. She was like the waves, gentle sometimes, raging the next, but forever going in and out, always to return.

"You may not want to continue our acquaintance if I tell you," he said finally. "It might be shocking."

"Oh, lord, you're not going to go on about propriety, are you? Excuse me if I have no pearls to clutch. Hypocrites, the lot of you. It doesn't matter what you do so long as the pretense is kept that you do not do it. Do you want to know who my husband was? I'll tell you. Before Abby, I worked as a maid for the fine house of Barmain. Yes, I can imagine you've heard of them. Their youngest son took a fancy to me, and I didn't mind him, but then Abby came along. His family forced us to marry and change our name. Then they threw us out. I was more than content to move on and be a 'widow.' All I asked of them was a mourning habit, but no. Never mind that the father had more maids on the hook than his three sons put together, and the mother ... she had a new man every other month, but they were always out of the gentry and she never got caught."

"Do other classes not do such things?"

"They do but not as much. Life is different when you have to work for your living. Not as much time to get bored."

Frederick laughed out loud. He wasn't sure he should but to have his life discussed so, it made it so much less heavy. Frederick told her everything. He talked about Margery, Cuthbert, all of it. He even talked of the melancholy and the stoics, and she listened. Ellie listened as if what he said was important. She nodded and hemmed but didn't interrupt. On and on he went until his throat was dry. He hadn't a clue where all of it came from, only now that it was all coming out, it could not be stopped. He told her about his mother, and how his mother loved Ovid and the statues in the garden. He tried not to look at her, either. He feared if he met her eye and she was bored or annoyed, it would all be over, but each time he glanced her way, she still listened.

After a time, he exhausted everything he could think of to say. He had never been more spent in all his life. Ellie handed him another sandwich and he took it gladly.

"Thank you," he said after he ate. "I've never been able to talk that much."

TO MASTER THE TIDES

"I know," said Ellie, laying a hand on his arm. The gentle weight of it eased his heart even more. Could there be any more peace than this?

Abby ran up to them, red in the face.

"Mama, can I have a sandwich?"

"Drink some water first," she said, holding the canteen for the little girl while Abby drank. She handed her half a sandwich and Abby picked up Zeus with the other hand.

"Did he behave?" she asked.

"He was very good," Frederick said.

"Are you sure?" asked Abby, cocking a wispy eyebrow. "He never behaves. But I like him just the same."

"It is good he has you, then," Frederick said. "I like him as well, mischievous or not. Now, I really must be going. Thank you, madame, for lunch and I hope we may speak again some time. I need to return the favor."

"Don't think of it that way," said Ellie, rising with him. "Shall we be friends? If you say so, friends listen to one another without expecting anything in return."

"Friends, then," he said, offering her his hand. She placed hers in his but said nothing else before he started back home.

Margery kept to her sitting room when Frederick got home. Cuthbert and Lucy were nowhere to be seen. Isabella gave him an earful about his hobo state. He took it and said nothing, ringing for a bath as soon as he got to his room. There was sand in every crevasse of his body. It was as if he rolled naked in it and shoveled it into orifices on purpose.

Waiting for the bath took some time. The Fittons' Brighton house still used copper tubs, none of the newfangled plumbing like some of the houses had. Frederick settled himself into the steaming water, careful to keep his hand out. The heat from the water seeped into his core and he never felt so invigorated. Was it the bath or was it from today, getting out some of that internal muck?

He would look for Ellie on the beach again tomorrow. Whatever she said, it was his turn to listen. With all the people he knew, everyone talked a great deal but fought over one another to be heard. Even Margery couldn't listen without telling him what he could have done better. Yes, he would look for Ellie again.

A servant knocked on the door. Frederick bid him enter.

"Forgive me, sir," said the footman. "This came for you. I thought it best to bring it directly."

A small package and a letter sat on his silver tray. He was right to bring it of course. Margery would tear into anything for him, especially how things were left. He thanked the man and hung over the edge of the tub to open the package. Inside was a shell. It was a smooth single whorl, salmon in color that deepened in the grooves. He tore open the letter next. The writing flowed in an elegant hand like the kinder ripples of the waves.

Mr. Estibus,

I hope I do not presume. Abby wanted you to have the shell as a thank you for finding Zeus. She should have thanked you properly before, but she is only six. Hopefully, she will learn better manners in time. She especially wanted me to tell you that this should protect you from the tides. Whether or not she overheard us talking or it is something she came up with on her own, I cannot say. She made me promise to tell you though, so promise kept.

TO MASTER THE TIDES

I am also writing to tell you this is goodbye, for now at least. We go back home this afternoon. I hadn't thought to say anything before. You'll forgive me but I did not realize how much I would enjoy your company. We live in the same town, I believe, and though we said as much earlier, I would be happy to keep up the acquaintance. Abby liked you and would be happy to see you again.

Until we speak again,
Ellie Miller

Frederick folded up the letter carefully, trying not to get it wet. He held up the shell and looked at it. It was perfect. Not a crack on it. It reminded him of Ellie, small and tough. He ought not to be thinking these kinds of things. Ellie was not like Margery. He believed Ellie when she said she wanted friendship and he ought not to betray that trust. Frederick hopped out of his bath and carefully wrapped the note and shell in some stockings and stowed them in the bottom of his travel trunk. He was sorry she was going but he would see her again. He felt better than he had in some time.

Ten

No one had seen Cuthbert for days now. There were signs in his room that he had been there. Dirty clothes piled up on the floor and other clothes missing. He came home to dress at least. Even without him, the room smelled of alcohol and vomit. Lucy wouldn't touch a thing, but Frederick was shameless about going through the pockets. Up one sleeve he found a few bent cards. Margery watched the whole process with a stoic expression.

"On a binge, again," she said. "Leave him be. He'll come home."

"But he's cheating again," Lucy sobbed. "He might not."

"Serves him right, then."

Frederick did not want to admit he felt the same. He usually just let Cuthbert be, but Lucy was so distraught, he conceded to go about town with her. She trailed behind him and waited on the street while he checked all the card houses he could find. Cuthbert had been at one of them the night before last but he lost all his money and was not welcomed back. Frederick sat Lucy down in a tearoom with a scone when he checked Madame's House. The ladies there flocked to Frederick. He dodged their wandering hands while he asked the Madame if Cuthbert had been by. She hadn't seen a man like that at all, but wouldn't he like to relieve some of his anxiety here? Frederick slipped away before any of the women could get hold of his manhood.

The last place to check was the jail. When Cuthbert wanted to gamble, there was no telling what ends he would go to. Frederick took Lucy back home for that visit, only saying he would keep looking. He needed to come up with a plausible excuse as to where Cuthbert was, should he turn up in jail.

Frederick took a moment in his room. His father usually handled this kind of thing. When Cuthbert was 17, old Lord Estibus had to come all the way back from London, to bail Cuthbert out. It was a pub fight that time and the other man got stabbed. He lived and admitted the knife started in his hand, so Cuthbert got off. Frederick suspected a lot of money ended up in the other man's hand rather than a knife starting there.

There was always a chance Cuthbert had thrown a fit and headed back to the country. Someone at the card house might have insulted him when he was losing. He did like to throw tantrums. Frederick rummaged through his chest. He wanted to find the shell, the talisman from the Fairy. He held it up in the light at his bedroom window, a brighter pink than he remembered. Seeing it reminded him of the day at the beach where no one demanded anything of anyone. The shell was imbued with the quiet. Yes, that was why it was so good. Company and real talk. Abby jumped and skipped and dug holes. With Cuthbert's children, at least one was always crying or tattling or shoving another down.

"Lend me some of your calm, today, will you?" said Frederick to the shell. He was only playing a trick on himself, but it seemed to work, nonetheless. He took a deep breath and imagined lying on the beach with the tides parting around him.

Once back in town, he had the carriage drop him off a few blocks away from the jailhouse. He wanted a walk. Though he was calm he still needed to muster the courage to go into the jail. How would he find his brother? No matter what his state, he would be difficult to move.

Frederick took the stone steps in front of the jailhouse as slowly as he could without drawing odd looks from passers-by. *Cuthbert, please don't be here, please.* He opened the door and went to the front desk. A long string of swearing followed by an out of tune, "Drink, and fill the night with mirth! Let us have a mighty measure." More swearing echoed from behind the door to the cells. *Shit.*

"Sorry 'bout him," said the bobby at the desk. "Can't get anything useful out of him, or else we'd send for his people."

"I'm afraid I am his people," said Frederick. His cheeks were burning hot already. "At least probably."

"You sure you want to claim him?"

"If he *is* my brother, I'm afraid I must."

Frederick cringed even more while the officer took down his information. The raving man had forgone the lyrics and was singing the swears now with a few cries of "shut it, you bloody tosser!" mingled in. The bobby led him through the door and down the hall between the cells.

"What's the smell," asked Frederick, putting a handkerchief to his nose.

"Bugger took a bloody rank shite the second we brought him in. This one smells fresh, though," said the bobby, gagging in his turn. "Bastard better be using the piss pot we gave him, they get those now, you see. More sanitary for everyone. Begging your pardon, sir."

Frederick shook his head, his eyes watering. Even after the childhood years of Cuthbert leaving them under his bed, he had never quite accustomed himself to the smell. At the door of Cuthbert's cell, Frederick peeped in. His brother pissed in the corner, still singing curses.

"He can't have been here long," said Frederick, "if he's still that drunk."

"Brought him in an hour or two ago. One of the men found him in front of a dice house on the dodgy end of town."

"And everyone already hates him? Never mind. What's his bail?"

"'Honestly, sir, we'll pay you if you take him."

Frederick shook his head and nodded for the bobby to let Cuthbert out.

"C'mon, man, pull your pants up," said the bobby as he opened the door.

"What, what? Little prig telling me what to do. I swear ... Frederick! Good show. Knew you'd come!" Cuthbert wiped his hands on his partially buttoned pants and tried to clap Frederick on the shoulder. Frederick dodged and Cuthbert stumbled.

"Come now, brother. Fix your clothes proper or you'll be back in here for indecency."

Frederick took a good look at Cuthbert while they waited on the street for a carriage to drive them back. He had been in a fight, surely. He had a black eye, and his lip was swollen. All the pockets on his jacket were ripped. Frederick could guess Cuthbert lost at dice and couldn't pay, but the odd things were the scratch marks on his cheeks. That was a woman's attack. Perhaps Cuthbert had tried the brothel on the dodgy end and couldn't pay there, either.

No matter. The carriage was here. Frederick, with the help of the footman and driver, hoisted Cuthbert into the compartment. Cuthbert laid down on the seat and fell asleep, drooling on the velvet cushion. The driver grumbled at him. Frederick sighed and flipped the man an extra bob.

"Where have you been?" Frederick asked. "Lucy was near frantic."

"Damn the woman. Damn all the women." Cuthbert dug his face deeper into the pillow.

"Were you at the dice house this whole time? That's new."

"They let me play on credit. The card places won't anymore. Father should give me more money."

"He doesn't because he knows you'll gamble it."

"I don't see why. It'll all be mine someday, anyhow."

"You're determined to rid yourself of it before you even get it? Good show, old boy. Who scratched your face?"

"Don't you have some bollox this morning?"

Frederick raised an eyebrow but said nothing. If Cuthbert didn't want to answer questions, he wouldn't. Frederick had hoped it was Lucy who had done it. It might still be. His brother would be embarrassed to be bested by his wife. Frederick might speak to Isabella about having Lucy stay for a bit after they left the Fittons. They would need to soon. Margery would not abide Cuthbert in this state for much longer. The trick was convincing Cuthbert of that. In his mind, he did no wrong.

TO MASTER THE TIDES

Fortunately for the driver, Cuthbert saved his vomit for the front steps of the Fittons. It took two footmen and the butler along with Frederick to get the man into his bed. Isabella watched the whole time. She found Frederick in the sitting room, napping in front of the hearth. He woke when she came in.

"I'm sorry," she said. "I only wanted to ask you something."

"You're no bother." It occurred to Frederick he *was* fond of Isabella. Perhaps if he weren't so wrapped up in his own troubles, they might have made a real go of it.

"Am I that bad?"

"At what?"

"I mean, I drink a frightful amount still. Am I as horrible as Cuthbert was when he came home?"

"Do you dice until they throw you out or take massive shites in the corner?"

Isabella's eyes widened in shock.

"I want to stop drinking. Maybe if I make a good example, Cuthbert could stop as well."

"I think Cuthy has more problems than alcohol," Frederick said, "but if you wish we can clear out the spirits at the house when we get home. I'm indifferent to it."

It truly was kind of her to want to influence his brother. Frederick felt it misplaced and useless, but if she could better herself in the process, so be it. He hadn't been fair to Isabella, really.

Frederick supposed he was bitter to her because he had no choice in marrying her. Her woes were because of him and his brother. When they got back, he would put in an effort. They needed friends other than Margery and Cuthbert. Poor Lucy should stay with them for a time as well. Yes, they would do so much when they got back. For now, he needed to get Cuthbert home. Isabella could stay with the Fittons for a bit. It wouldn't do to subject her to the inevitable fit his brother would throw on the way home.

Undeterred by his jailing, Cuthbert continued his bender. Frederick came downstairs to his brother throwing a fit in the sitting room and drinking directly from the brandy bottle. Lucy cried in a chair in the corner. Margery stood behind Cuthbert, watching him like a lioness stalking her prey. Isabella stood before him, biting her lip and clenching her fists. She was red in the face but looked ashamed rather than angry or tearful.

"Dammm-ned women. All look alike," said Cuthbert, looming over the tiny Isabella. "You should've ... you. It's your fault. Damn you."

Frederick was no stranger to this sort of fit. His father threw them all the time, screaming at nothing, blaming their mother for something he did himself.

It was all down to their mother that the fortune stayed together. They had a good lawyer, and she was good at getting their father to sign things when he was drunk. It was she who secured her brother's money for Frederick and the Estibus money for Cuthbert. Once that was done, she died.

Frederick often thought his mother only willed herself to live until that was done. There was no good diagnosis of why she died. She only wasted away in her bed, too weak to lift a finger or see anyone.

Cuthbert now railed on, not at his wife, but Frederick's.

"Why didn't you say anything?!" Cuthbert yelled at Isabella. "It was you. You wanted me to. You let me."

TO MASTER THE TIDES

Frederick looked to Margery to see what had happened. Whatever it was, he was sure Isabella wasn't to blame. Isabella looked at Frederick, her face blanched and eyes wide. In that face, he saw his mother all over again, too terrified to even cry. His father never hit her, but he didn't have to.

It was like that with Frederick's melancholy. It was not that other feelings weren't there, that he was as stoic as stone, it was that the other feelings were always bottled and put away. There was never the right moment to let them out. They bubbled to the top now, good time or no.

"Cuthbert!"

"And what the deuce do you have to say to me, little brother."

Frederick punched Cuthbert in the mouth and sent him reeling into a side table. Knickknacks shattered on the parquet floor. Cuthbert sat dazed where he was, neck of the broken brandy bottle still in hand.

"You're being a cunt," said Frederick, ignoring Cuthbert's outstretched hand. "You always were one, for as long as I can remember. Your tantrums aren't manly. You need to grow up."

Cuthbert looked from Isabella to Lucy to Margery. None of them made a move to help him up. After a few shaky attempts, he managed to haul his girth to his feet. He stared at Frederick a moment with only one focused eye and then burst out into a fit of laughter. It wasn't merry. The maniacal tones chilled Frederick to the core.

"You," Cuthbert said, pointing at his brother. "You. You'll see. If you only knew the things I knew."

"Cuthy, do shut it," said Margery.

JOSEPHINE BORGIA

"And you, you trollop," Cuthbert went to Margery and grabbed her by the throat and chin. "What a mess you always create. Knew we shouldn't have come here."

How collected Margery looked in the face of it all. It was almost more frightening than Cuthbert's rage. He was mostly fat, but his grip was still like iron tongs. Frederick hauled him away by the collar. Margery's cheeks were still red. There would be bruising.

"We're going home," Frederick said to his brother. "Go have your servants pack. If you won't, I'll tell them."

"You're the big man now, are you?"

Frederick punched him again in the face—and in the stomach. Cuthbert doubled over on the floor and stayed there for a moment, before vomiting. Margery ran for the footmen.

"Get him upstairs," she said. "Take care he doesn't bleed on any of the carpets."

The servants had Frederick and Cuthbert packed in good time. Frederick had already ordered the coach and waited in the sitting room with some scotch for Cuthbert to haul his fat arse downstairs. Margery sat with him. They didn't talk at first. The last fight had been a bad one but so it was with them. Margery looked as if she wanted to make up already.

"Must you really go?" she asked.

"Cuthbert must. Don't you think that Lucy needs a break from him? It was good of you to keep her on. Isabella, too. I feel she could always use a break from me."

"But you."

"You know Cuthbert. He'll get in the coach all right but who knows where he'll get out. We might lose him for a month."

TO MASTER THE TIDES

"Not a sad loss."

"Lucy is still fond of him in spite of everything." They sat quiet a moment. "What was Cuthbert yelling at Isabella for?"

Margery eyed Frederick a moment before she spoke. "His fault, really."

"Always is."

"He came in, well, you saw how drunk he was, and Isabella was napping on the sofa. It seems he 'mistook' Isabella for Lucy. He was leaning down to kiss her when Lucy walked in. The ungodly mess you saw was the result."

"Do you really think Cuthbert 'mistook' Isabella?"

Margery didn't answer and Frederick didn't push it. Cuthbert was capable of anything when he was drunk. In some ways, he was worse than their father. Cuthbert was spoiled and indulged all his life. Their father never showed him affection, but he never punished him, either. Cuthbert was always good at making jokes at the expense of others and that was the only thing that got a laugh out of Estibus Sr. Their mother was the only one who could handle Cuthbert. She never yelled and in her gentle way always got him to behave. Cuthbert's drinking and gambling started after she died.

Frederick dearly missed his mother. When he was small, the melancholy was there even then. She was the only one who didn't scold him for it. He suspected that was because she had it herself.

He missed the days when he was a child. There was a swing on the porch of their home. On the worst days, she would take him there, just the two of them, away from the noise of their father and Cuthbert. They watched the birds and the squirrels and share a cup of tea or cocoa. They never had to talk about anything, just be. His mother was the wind that kept the tides back. It was odd how the wind could do that, as powerful as the waves were, the wind could whip them where they liked.

A servant came in the room and cleared his throat.

"Begging your pardon, Lady Fitton. The coach is here but the gentleman won't come down."

"Bring him down," said Margery. She sounded weary. "Use as many men as you need and if that doesn't work, send for the police. Do not worry about being polite to the man. We're tossing him out, after all."

"Are you going to strip him naked," asked Frederick, snickering. "Fortunate for Cuthbert there is no snow."

Great bangs and bumps thundered from upstairs. Furniture scraped along the hard floor, punctuated by Cuthbert's swearing, echoed through the floorboards. The yelling continued while Frederick and Margery listened. Frederick was about to get up to assist the servants when all of a sudden, the noise stopped, and they heard nothing further.

"Did they kill him?" asked Frederick.

"I hope not. I told them not to let him bleed on anything."

Someone came down the stairs, but it was not Frederick. It was Isabella in her traveling cloak.

"I'm all packed, too," she said. "Cuthbert is calm. He will come with us."

"Do you not want to stay on with the ladies?" Frederick asked. He wasn't going to oppose whatever Isabella wanted to do but he felt for her having to endure a hungover Cuthbert for a long carriage ride.

"I will go where my husband goes," she said. "Besides, I think Lucy is still under some misunderstanding of the situation she walked in on. I leave it to Margery to clear things up. Then I will try to mend our friendship. I will not apologize. I did nothing wrong. I'll leave the apologies to Cuthbert."

The servants loaded up the coach with everyone's belongings. Mercifully, Cuthbert passed out early on into the ride, taking up the entire seat on his side. Frederick and Isabella stared out their respective windows. Soon, Frederick was out himself. He only woke once before they stopped at an inn for the night. He said nothing, but in the waning sunlight, he thought Isabella looked softer. She had a small grin on her face as she watched the countryside slip by, and he wondered what she thought of. She looked genuinely happy. He was glad for it. Marrying him hadn't completely ruined her life. There had to be something more he could do for her.

As he drifted back off, his dreams, however, turned to Ellie. They walked on the beach together, the water barricaded away from them with a wall full of salmon shells.

"You've found me in your dreams," she said. "The contract is complete now. Take care not to break the shell."

She held out her arms to him.

"I can't," he said but slipped into them anyway. He nestled his head into her shoulder and wept. Did she smell so good in real life or did his dreams imagine it? *This must be real love, it must, it must, it must.*

He awoke in the carriage to Isabella shaking his arm. It was night. The coach driver held a lantern outside the open coach door. Cuthbert was gone.

"He's already inside, snoring in his room," said Isabella. "Our things are in, too. It was a shame to wake you."

JOSEPHINE BORGIA

Frederick nodded and wiped the drool from his chin. He wobbled a bit, still groggy but followed Isabella into the inn.

Eleven

Isabella got them a room at a fancy inn. It was a small town between Brighton and the country, but many people stopped there, and the inn prospered. Once Cuthbert was stashed, Frederick and Isabella went to the dining room for dinner. It was every bit as nice as anything you would find in London or Bath or New York even. The maître d' sat them at a loft table overlooking low hills covered in trees. Some of the trees flowered.

Steaks for dinner. Flambe for dessert. Frederick wasn't sure how he was going to get up he stuffed himself so. He could see why Isabella liked this sort of thing. They talked during dinner easier than they had in a long time. They were fed and it was quiet, and they had plenty of wine and scotch to sustain them. Isabella could hold her liquor very well.

"Cuthbert truly was atrocious, don't you think?" Isabella said. "I don't know what he was thinking behaving in such a way."

"We overstayed our welcome, I think," said Frederick, lighting a cigarette in the candle on the table. Most places were going to electricity now, or at least had gas lights. This place, while fancy, still had candles on the tables and in the chandeliers. Frederick liked it. It reminded him of when he was a boy and tides were still kind to him.

JOSEPHINE BORGIA

"Margery didn't care. She gets bored without company."

"I mean, we overstayed for Cuthbert. He can be civil and keep his bad habits in order, for a time, but they always get the better of him. I couldn't tell you what drives him to do it."

Isabella frowned. Frederick didn't ask what was wrong. She would tell him if she wanted him to know. She didn't. They sat for a bit more and Frederick made a move to signal for the check, but Isabella stopped him.

"Can we sit for just a moment more?" she asked. "We go to these kinds of places so little."

"Would you like anything else?"

A mischievous smile crept across Isabella's face. "Do you think I could get that piece of chocolate cake we saw on the dessert cart?"

"We've already had dessert, but if you think you have room."

He flagged down the waiter and ordered two glasses of champagne, no wait, bring the bottle. They weren't celebrating anything, but they had made it through a trip without fighting or nettling each other. Isabella's drinking had confined itself to social events and Frederick felt good. Simply good. Not euphoric as he had in his first days with Margery and certainly not as good as when he was a child, but the melancholy lifted.

Halfway into the bottle, they still talked and got along better than they had, since, well, ever.

"I was proud of the way you dealt with Cuthbert," said Isabella, finishing off the last bite of cake. She ate the whole thing by herself.

"Someone should have done it years ago. *I* should have done it years ago."

TO MASTER THE TIDES

"Will Lucy carry on with him, do you think? It's much easier to get a divorce now. Margery will bear witness to his abuse and Fitton will, too. He does whatever she says."

"They're both from old stock," said Frederick, staring into his glass, watching the bubbles. "Neither of them would do it."

"That makes you from old stock, too."

"No. I'm more like my mother was."

"Tell me about her."

Frederick poured more champagne and obliged. He told Isabella how his mother reminded him of a cherry blossom. Pale pink, she looked almost white but there was color there if you knew where to look. The sea was always calm for her whenever they went. Once, they took the carriage there in a rain shower. Frederick was 6 and cried the whole way there. Cuthbert was disappointed, too, but didn't dare take it out on Frederick while their mother was there. She only laughed and said, "You'll see." The sun came out when they got to the beach and it was much cooler than it had been all day before. It was a fun day. She was still happy then. Frederick couldn't say when the change was, but it was only a little after that.

Isabella laid a hand on Frederick's arm.

"I'm sorry," she said. "I wish I could have met your mother."

"She would have liked you," he said. "Two bright suns lighting up the sky."

"Is that what you think of me?"

"Didn't I tell you? That's what I thought when I first saw you. I worried my shadows might put you out, and they did in a way. I'm sorry for that."

"Don't worry. I could have done worse." A shadow clouded Isabella's face.

JOSEPHINE BORGIA

"Are you thinking of Lucy?" asked Frederick. "I couldn't tell you how many are out there like Cuthbert. I used to think that's what a man was supposed to be, and I never measured up. It was daunting to be like Cuthbert all the time, takes too much energy. My father is proud of him, though, for what I don't know. The more I see of the world, I'm glad I'm not like him."

"Yes, I was thinking of Lucy," said Isabella, smiling now. Her eyes swam a little, but Frederick barely saw it, his eyes were swimming, too. "How well you seem to know me now, Freddy. Where was this when we were first married?"

"Freddy now, is it? I don't know."

"Shall we take the rest of the champagne to our room?"

Frederick laughed.

"Yes, let's."

They stayed up far later into the night than Frederick ever thought. Isabella, though drunk, was happier than she had been in a long time. They talked of frivolous things, and family things, and things they did as children. Frederick had never had a night like this with Margery. They certainly laughed together but she was always trying to educate him about one thing or another or complaining that he mussed her hair. Isabella didn't care about that. When Frederick reached for the ties of Isabella's dress, she did not stop him.

After the second go, they lay in bed with the window cracked. It was hot in the room and the sheets got twisted about. The cool air on their sticky skin was like ambrosia to the tongue. They were both a little more sober now, but the glow of the evening hadn't worn off.

TO MASTER THE TIDES

"You mentioned divorce earlier," said Isabella. "Do you want one?"

"No. What would you do? I couldn't leave you like that. It's not so accepted in our county as it is in the city. Do you want one?"

"No," she said, almost too quiet to hear. "I don't."

Frederick woke up the next morning shivering. Isabella had pulled all the covers to her side. Frederick got up, still naked, and closed the window. He put on a dressing robe and sat at the toilet table. His head pounded. He wanted to ring for some hair of the dog or some laudanum, but Isabella wasn't dressed yet, and a breast hung out of the covers. Was he allowed to look? Ought he to look? He understood marriage so little, his own especially. Margery once told him she had never seen Lord Fitton nor he, her. They always left on a nightshirt. "Doesn't that get tangled?"

"It never lasts long enough to tangle anything up." Was that better than nothing at all?

Last night was certainly a surprise. He had never thought of reconciling with Isabella, but what would be the harm? She didn't love him. Even when they were very drunk, Frederick could tell that, but if they could enjoy each other's company, the years together might be pleasant. He was glad she could still have fun. At dinner, she reminded him of the girl he first met.

"You're still in there, aren't you," he said, reaching to brush some hair off her face.

At the touch, Isabella awoke with a start. Frederick wondered at the fear in her eyes, but it passed as soon as she woke enough to realize where she was.

"I'm sorry. I ..."

"Oh, don't look," she yelled, wincing and rubbing her temples.

"Headache? Me, too. Shall I ring for ..."

Isabella got up, eyes wide and frantic. Searching the room, she grabbed up a wastebasket and vomited into it. It didn't hold the vomit well and Frederick handed her a piss pot from under the bed. Isabella knelt on the floor after she finished and sat with her eyes closed.

"Remind me never to drink champagne again," she said. Frederick laughed and went to pat her on the shoulder, but she put up a hand to keep him off. "Let's go. The smell in here won't be gone before we leave. I'd rather wait for Cuthbert in the lobby."

Servants came to clear out the mess and help them pack up, but Cuthbert beat them downstairs. He had slept since yesterday and, he looked fresh and jolly.

"What were the two of you up to?" he said when he saw them. "You should have got me up." Cuthbert pouted.

"Yes, we were drinking without you," said Frederick. "Don't be a child about it."

"So, you're still Mr. Big today, are you? I wondered where that came from."

"I don't know what you mean," said Frederick. "But if you plan on being an ass, I'm going to keep telling you about it."

"Well, that's not kind of him," Cuthbert said to Isabella. "He should show his brother more respect."

Isabella did not seem to be in the mood for Cuthbert at the moment and opened her mouth to say something sharp but instead of words out of her mouth, it was vomit. Cuthbert leapt back just in time, red in the face. Frederick interrupted him before he could start swearing.

"Sorry," said Frederick. "Champagne. You know how it is." And he helped Isabella outside, leaving his brother to tell someone about being sick on the carpet.

Frederick took the shell out first when he got his things up to his room at home. He didn't want the servants to touch it, though he couldn't say why. He believed that it was what gave him strength, silly as it sounded. Perhaps it was magic from the fairy. Or maybe that it was simply being able to do something that made two people happy, small as it was. It gave him the courage to try with others. He preferred to believe the former. Frederick thanked the shell and placed it in his desk drawer. He didn't feel it was safe anywhere else.

He ought to write Ellie straight away to thank Abby for the gift. He should have done that in Brighton but amid the business with Cuthbert, he had forgotten all about it. He sat down and pulled out some paper and turned the shell this way and that on the shelf in front of him. He had noticed its salmon color but now he saw streaks that were a darker red. Had it been that way before? He touched it with a finger and made another wish. "Perhaps I could find love," he said out loud. He thought of the night before with Isabella. It would be pleasant to have a life like that with her. There were plenty of people in arranged marriages who grew to care for one another. Why not him? He knew very well it was his fault it hadn't happened before. Now he felt as if it could.

Downstairs, Frederick inquired with the housekeeper if Mrs. Estibus had come back down yet. No, she was still abed, not feeling well. That was to be expected, Frederick supposed.

JOSEPHINE BORGIA

The champagne had not sat well with her and the journey had been rough. Neither she nor he was able to take a nap with Cuthbert's yammering. He was back to his old jolly self as if the episode in Brighton had never happened. Frederick was thankful that it happened there, where they had few acquaintances. He went to the sitting room and fell asleep in a stuffed chair by the fire. The next thing he knew, a maid woke him for tea.

Frederick sipped his tea alone. He debated on going to see how Isabella was. Normally, he left her alone but after the stay at the inn, he was curious if she wanted to see him. He nibbled on a biscuit and waffled back and forth. The servant came in with a fresh pot. Frederick opened his mouth and closed it again.

"Have we any coffee?" he asked, finally.

"No, sir. Shall I ask cook to order some sir?"

"Yes, do."

Frederick chewed his thumbnail.

After tea, he went to his room. He had forgotten the letter to Ellie. It was written and sealed but still sat on his desk. He paused as he reached for it, watching the shell.

"Give me courage, little thing. I do want love this time."

He shoved the letter to Ellie in his pocket and went to check on Isabella.

The door to Isabella's room creaked a little when it opened but she didn't wake. She slept sound, snoring loudly, her face half-buried in the pillow. Frederick crept over to her bed and squatted down next to it to get eye level with her.

"Cuthbert, you arse," she muttered.

TO MASTER THE TIDES

Even in her sleep, she dislikes him. Frederick chuckled to himself. He reached out and brushed her hair away from her face as he did at the inn but unfortunately it had the same result as before. Isabella gasped and sat straight up in bed.

"Frederick, what are you doing in here?"

"I wanted to see how you're feeling," he said, worried a bit by her tone. "You can call me Freddy if you like. It was pleasant to hear the other day."

"I feel just awful, still," she said, eying him. "Let me sleep."

"Do you need anything? Shall I have them bring you some tea?"

"No, I'm fine."

Frederick didn't say anything else, but he didn't go either. He was deflated somewhat. What had he expected? To crawl into bed with her? He didn't want to do anything except maybe wake up warm the way he had that morning. Warm and not alone. Why did men and women sleep in separate rooms, even when the congress was sanctioned? If they did share a bed every night, would they be closer or tired of each other? It was all too maddening to think about. He had been so stupid.

"Did you need something, Frederick?" asked Isabella. "I'm sorry," she said taking his hand. "I know we had a jolly time last night, but I was very drunk. I hope I didn't ... I hope I didn't lead you to believe anything that ..."

"No," said Frederick. He yanked his hand away harder than he meant. "No, I'm sorry. I didn't mean to bother you while you were resting."

"Frederick, don't be like that." But he had already turned to walk out the door.

JOSEPHINE BORGIA

Frederick took the carriage to town. Out in the street, he strode along, not minding where he was going, muttering and cursing under his breath.

"Deuced fool I am and always have been. Embarrassment. What is wrong with me? Such a damned fool." Those thoughts came again, as they did when he was hard on himself. *I should have just ... No. I wasn't meant to die then. Abby and Ellie are safe because of me. Maybe someday, but not then and not now. I can't disappoint them yet, and they would be so disappointed in me.*

Rain splashed cold on his neck. Before long, he was nearly soaked and realized he didn't know where he was. Pulling his hat tight over his ears, he paused under a street sign. He had meant to head to the post office to post the letter, but he hadn't paid any heed to where he was going. He stopped at the corner and checked the street sign. Hephzibah and Troilus: that wasn't far from Ellie's address. He could walk it there much quicker. He put up his collar against the steady rain and made a dash for it.

A cold drip from the awning of Ellie's building found Frederick's neck no matter which way he stepped. After a moment or two, he gave up trying to force himself to ring the bell. The letter had gotten soaked in his mad dash to the building. Now, he just stood there, dumbly staring at the ruined note in his hand, ink bleeding through and dripping on the pavement.

The door opened and out came Ellie, bumping straight into him. Frederick teetered on the top step as if frozen in space before Ellie grabbed his coat sleeve and pulled him back from the brink. Frederick sputtered and coughed, unsure of how to explain himself.

"Mr. Estibus, you're wet through," she said, fairly shrieking at him. "Come up to the flat and warm up."

"But you were going out ..."

"Only going for a cuppa while Abby has her lesson. Come, come. If you get ill on my account, I shall feel very sorry indeed."

Ellie lived in a flat on the third floor of the building. The stairwell up smelled like very old wooden furniture that had been in the attic for a bit, musty and mothballed. Inside the apartment was much brighter. It had a small foyer with a parlor to the left and a hall leading to the other rooms to the right. The coat rack by the door seemed new. The hooks and wood paneling were in that swooping Nouveau style that was starting to pop up all over the place. The rugs were old, though, but well cared for, and baskets of potpourri chased off the must from the stairwell. From one of the back rooms, piano notes tinkled their way up the hall. It was a childish tune, tapped out in more staccato than it was likely meant to be, but the notes were there and in time. It had a shy quality to the sound and Frederick could imagine tiny fairy fingers touching each key and darting away.

"Is that Abby?" asked Frederick as Ellie took his hat and shook out his coat. "She sounds promising."

"I think she has a good ear," Ellie said. "She lacks confidence. Come this way. There is another small sitting room over here. I'll have them bring more wood for the fire."

JOSEPHINE BORGIA

"Are you sure?" asked Frederick. It had just occurred to him that he went up to a woman's flat on his own. "I mean, I should have objected. It's not proper I'm here."

Ellie raised an eyebrow at him.

"What exactly are you implying, sir?"

"Nothing against you, of course. I mean, one must be careful of how things might look, and I wouldn't want to ..."

Ellie laughed gently at his blubbering.

"I'm teasing you. My brother Stanway lives here as well. Father wasn't so kind to him in the will, so I took him in. You might meet him, or maybe not. He sleeps most of the day. I'm starting to think that father was right in calling him a layabout."

The two went into the drawing room and Frederick sat in a chair by the fire. Ellie rang the bell and took the chair across from his.

"So, Mr. Estibus," she began, pulling tobacco pouch out of a pocket on the side of the chair. "I'm sorry, do you mind?"

"No, not at all."

"My goodness, you look like a starving vulture. Would you like one?"

Frederick nodded. He had never seen a person roll a cigarette so deftly in his life, and they were even, too, tobacco packed snug.

"They taste so much better when you roll them right," she said, lighting his cigarette with her own. "Forgive me. I am pleased to see you but worry that there is something amiss for you to dash all the way here in the rain."

"No," said Frederick, even more shy now that he had to explain himself. "I meant to post a note, announce myself that I was back in town, you know, but I got lost, and since I was so close, I thought to stick the letter in the mail slot myself, but then I got caught in the rain..." He trailed off and glanced at her side-eye, taking a drag off the cigarette she gave him. It *was* good, especially without the little bits of tobacco escaping into your mouth.

"Oh, dear," Ellie laughed out loud, but it wasn't cruel or condescending. If Frederick didn't know any better the look in her eye was almost affectionate. "You are such a noodle! You needn't adhere to all the old rules with me. I think we're past standing on ceremony at this point, don't you think?"

"We barely know one another," Frederick muttered, staring at his knee.

"There's time for that, of course," said Ellie. "But I trust you, Mr. Estibus, so that has to count for something."

Frederick looked her in the face and in her eye, the connection was back. Animal to animal, breathing along together in the live world, except this time she wasn't frightened and alone, and her trust in him was not that of a child's. She didn't need him for anything, and he could not harm her in any way, but she had faith in him. She could hurt him, however, not overtly, she would never do a cruel thing on purpose, but she had power over him now and could slash him to the quick if she wanted.

"How is your hand?" she asked. "It was a very nasty burn when I saw it. You still have it bandaged. Shall we take a look?"

Frederick shot to his feet. He didn't want to be reminded of Margery just now, or ever, really. That's why he left the bandage on. It was as if Ellie protected him from her. He didn't realize it, though, until just this moment.

JOSEPHINE BORGIA

"I must go," he said. "I'm warm now and the rain has eased up. Thank you for your hospitality."

Ellie looked surprised but stood with him.

"It was no trouble," she said. "You will come again?"

"Yes, of course. I'd like to meet your brother."

Frederick gave a few more awkward nods and dashed out the door.

Twelve

Frederick berated himself all the way home. It did not stop raining and he got soaked all over again. He was chilled to the bone when he got home. Even more so than when Margery threw him in the snow. There was a certain degree of numbness that went along with being frozen. When that wore off, it turned to pain. This time he was cold, body and soul.

He sat in front of the fire in his room, wrapped in a blanket, rehashing the whole damnable episode. Until he embarrassed himself, he had not realized how much he wanted to see the heart-shaped face, the delicate fae-fingers that could roll a smoke so perfectly. What else could she do with those hands? It was better this way. He thought about her too much already. If she turned him away it would be easy to forget her.

It was time to take off the bandage. On top was a memory of Ellie, underneath was Margery. It was her mark. He was trapped forever, was he not? He pushed her away, but she always came back in, like the tide itself. He touched the bandages, one last time and unwound them, not wanting to look at his hand. The bandages went on the fire, but instead of smoking smelled of morning glories. Agh, the ointment that Ellie put on him. She would not let him forget.

He inhaled deep and relished the scent for a moment. He ought not to let himself indulge. Finally, Frederick looked to his hand. How deeply had Margery branded him? But the wound had healed entirely. No scar or trace of any kind remained. Frederick went to the window to get a better look. The sun was not out but it was bright enough. He was healed. Ellie ought to package and sell the ointment. She would never worry for money again. "Fae cream," she could call it. People had enough sense now to not go about burning people for witchcraft, didn't they?

Frederick settled in front of the fire. He had a book or two with him but did not feel like reading. His desk was open, and the shell sat in a pigeonhole. He asked the shell for love but wasn't specific about from whom or what kind.

Ellie might send love to everyone as a mother does a child. But Frederick couldn't think of her that way. He thought of the sweet face and the ever-present consciousness in the eyes. They summed him up and judged but somehow didn't hate him even though he suspected she saw completely through him. With everything he was, she still wished to know him. Well, maybe not after today.

Thank you, he thought to the shell. Thank you for not being a monkey's paw with my wishes. He ought to write to Ellie, to apologize for leaving so quickly but he was too embarrassed. Still, he felt better. After enough time passed, he could greet her again on the street. Yes, everything would be well. He needed a little time to forget the curves of her heart-shaped face.

At dinner that night, Frederick was back to himself again, or rather his new self. Isabella did not feel well but she plodded through dinner just the same. Frederick was feeling gregarious for once in his life and actually itched to talk.

TO MASTER THE TIDES

"May Day is coming up," he said.

"Yes, it is," said Isabella, sipping her wine.

"I know we've missed the Fittons' festivities for years now, but would you like to go this year?" The Fittons always hosted May Day on their grounds. The entire town was invited, from the lowest to the highest; even the servants were encouraged to take their turns in the festivities.

"Will Margery be in town?" Isabella asked. "After Cuthbert's nonsense, she may never want to see him again."

"Cuthbert always has nonsense. Everyone knows it and no one will judge us for it."

"Hmmm, well, why did you want to go?"

Frederick thought a moment. Because I want to see Ellie. He couldn't tell his wife that, no matter what their circumstances, even if Ellie was only a friend. Isabella wouldn't understand.

"I don't know," he said. "I'm tired of moping about the house. I thought you would be pleased."

"We can go if you like," Isabella said. "I would prefer not to see your brother if it can be helped."

"Lucy will be disappointed."

"I'll see her gladly."

"Fine. I promise to drag Cuthbert off to the beer garden and leave him there."

Isabella was feeling better the day of the festival. The sun shone bright, and a gentle breeze kept up, weaving its way among the party-goers. The Fitton grounds were a sea of pavilions, each one with a theme: beer, wine, roast boar, roast foul, barbecue, and on and on. The Maypole rose up in the clearing in the center. Winding its ribbons would be the highlight for the children. An orchestra played up closer to the house where a dance floor lay. The grounds teemed with people, but everything was so spread out, it was hardly crowded.

The Estibuses arrived close to noon, Isabella rosy and smiling on Frederick's arm. He meant them to be friends at least. Even if she hadn't meant the night at the Inn, it had brought them closer. He felt he could be himself around her and he was thankful for it.

"Let me know if you feel horribly," Frederick said. "I know you've been unwell of late. We don't have to stay if you aren't enjoying yourself."

"I'll be fine, Frederick, but I would like to sit."

They searched the tents until they found Margery with Lucy and Mrs. Whetherton in the barbecue tent, all making an awful mess of the napkins they had tied around their necks. Mrs. Whetherton complained of the heat (though it wasn't hot), the servants (though they always seemed to be at her elbow), and the crowds (which were not so very bad, except perhaps under the beer tent.) One couldn't take her seriously, however, with the quantity of barbecue sauce on her face.

"Do you wish to sit here?" whispered Frederick. "It might be tiresome."

"It will be fine," said Isabella wilting into a chair. "Will you fetch me some food."

Frederick hurried to do so. Her burst of energy had not lasted long. After he delivered the plate, he nodded to each of the ladies in turn. Margery extended her hand to him with a wry smile. As she pleased. He gave her the one she tried to brand and left it there, returning her smirk. Her face stayed blank, but she saw. *You see,* he thought, *I'm not yours after all.*

Isabella dismissed him so she might chat with the ladies. Frederick stuffed his hands in his pockets and headed for the beer tent. The men there were already fair lubricated and laughing raucously. Cuthbert was nowhere to be seen. Frederick got himself a stout and joined the group of laughing men. He knew a few from his club. He spotted Kilkenny's bright red hair among them. Irishman, but not a bad chap for all that.

"Got yerself a pint o' the plain, I see," said Kilkenny when Frederick joined them. "We've had a morning already and no mistake."

"Oh?"

"Old Cuthy was here, but he's already screwed the pooch for the day and went home."

Frederick's heart sank and he took a long drink of his stout. "What did he do?"

"Well, do you see that woman over there, drinking down her plain?"

Frederick looked. The men were crowded around Ellie, who sat with another man who could only be her brother. He had the same heart-shaped face and delicate build. He looked only a boy, but his eyes were circled from too much drink, and they had that same look as Ellie's—deep, but his seemed haunted.

"What happened with her?" Frederick asked.

"Her name's Mrs. Miller. Widow, I think. Fair looking bird if you ask me. Cuthy must have thought so, too, but she turned him down flat. He went on one of his raves about how women ought not to be in the beer tent at all. Well, she looked at him, cool as anything, pinched his fat cheek and said, 'Neither should children, yet here you are,' and she finished her plain as quick as lightning and ordered another.

"All the men got a good laugh out of that, and you know that didn't sit well with your brother. No one would help him, though, how could you? A lady such as that will win any day, and he went off in a huff, the silly bugger."

"Probably for the best," said Frederick, smiling to himself.

Ellie spotted him and waved.

"Do ya know the lass?" Kilkenny asked.

"We've met a few times," Frederick replied.

"Mr. Estibus! Well met," she said as she came towards them.

Frederick did the introductions, and Ellie smiled up at them both. Her eyes swam a little, but she still had full control of her faculties.

"Pleased to meet you, Mr. Kilkenny," she said. "My daughter dropped her favorite bear in town not too long ago, and Mr. Estibus was kind enough to pick him up and return him."

"How are Abby and Zeus?" Frederick asked.

"Abby is extremely well and Zeus is as filthy as ever," said Ellie, "but she won't let me get a hand on him to wash him. I fight my battles where I can. Would you like to say hello to her? She's playing with the other children but I'm sure she'll want to see you."

The two took their leave of Kilkenny and left their empty pints behind. Ellie offered Frederick a smoke from her case as they walked, and he took it gladly.

"You'll need to show me the trick of rolling these," said Frederick, taking an appreciative drag.

TO MASTER THE TIDES

"You can't," she said. "Your fingers are too fat. You'll have to come to me for one if want one. Now, Frederick," she said, pausing and turning to him, "have you recovered from our last meeting?"

Frederick assumed he must have looked horrified because Ellie burst into hysterical laughter.

"I'm sorry," she said. "Your face. I forget how constrained you gentry types are. I hope you'll forgive my vulgar merchant-class habits. Please do not worry about those kinds of things with me. As long as you're always kind to me and Abby, I have no quarrel with you."

It was such an odd feeling for Frederick. He felt so free, as if the weights dragging him down were suddenly loosed and sinking to the bottom of the ocean without him. He could see them, in his mind's eye, falling, falling, falling to the depths with the Kraken. He burst out laughing.

"I'm such a stuffed pig, Mrs. Miller. I should be asking your forgiveness."

"Call me Ellie, please. You've seen more of me than most men have. It seems too formal."

Frederick turned beet red but still ...

"Ellie," he whispered, trying it out.

They finished their smoke and came to where the children played. Abby waved at them both but showed no signs of wanting to come over. Ellie and Frederick walked on and Frederick didn't mind it a bit. He listened as Ellie talked as she would, giving a word of encouragement here and there to keep her going. She talked of her first home by the sea, where she would see her father off on his ship to France and Spain and once to India. Her mother left when her brother was very little.

JOSEPHINE BORGIA

When her father came back from India, he brought a bride with him. She tired of him as quickly as the cold winters and left him not much after.

Ellie tried several times to pry information out of Frederick, but he would not be drawn to talk. He much preferred to hear her. She went on for a little but soon they fell into a comfortable silence. They went on, far away from the crowd. Frederick knew where they were going but he was ashamed to admit how he knew. Margery had a private garden amongst tall hedges. He went there with her only once. The statues in there were of Greek myth again. He could only imagine his father's generation trying to outdo each other with the number of gods they called to their banner. Poseidon lived here, too. Margery didn't care for Frederick's insolence when he came near the statue, so she only took him here once. Pert, she called him. Frederick thought on that now and decided she didn't like it when he had his own power. He wanted to show Ellie the statue, wanted that more than anything he had ever wanted in his life.

"Come this way," he said. "I'll tell you something about myself."

Frederick led Ellie through the maze of bushes and statues. It wasn't a formal maze, but one could get lost easily. It was another world in the hedge-lined garden. He had brought Margery only once early in the relationship when he thought himself in love but was still such a child. He wanted Margery to see the Poseidon fountain in the center as he saw it. He loved it when he came here as a child with his father. Poseidon again!

Young Frederick thought the god followed him everywhere. The truth of the matter was, that 50 or so years ago, a sculptor had come through the borough who was a better salesman than an artist. He could only do Poseidon, so everyone in the county had one. Frederick's father had been especially taken in, commissioning one for the London home as well.

Eight-year-old Frederick knew nothing of this. Adding to the confusion, all the statues had the same misplaced brow line, drawn too close to the eyes. The sculptor likely fancied this made the god look fierce. In reality, it made him look an unfortunate caveman. Frederick liked his troglodyte protector all the same, even now, and he wanted to show it to Ellie. She might be the only person who would not laugh at him. Frederick told her the story, but she didn't laugh at him once, only asked to see the work itself. Frederick planned on taking a leisurely walk but when she insisted, he took her straight there.

"My heart warms to the poor fellow," said Ellie, crossing her arms and studying the statue as if she were appraising fine art.

"Mine too," Frederick said, "but don't pity him. He can take care of himself."

"Can he? I'm glad." She took a seat on the bench in an arbor across from the statue. Frederick wished she hadn't. It was where Margery *did* laugh at him when he told her the same thing. He sat next to her, anyway.

It was cool under the arbor and the morning glories that grew overhead smelled of ambrosia. Ellie sat there breathing it in with her eyes closed. She looked entirely happy. Frederick wondered what that felt like. He had moments in his life, but the melancholy was always there, like a shadow in the corner of his eye. He could never quite get a look at it or catch it creeping in, and before he was aware, it was on him. Now he didn't know what he felt. He watched Ellie's content face and envied it, loved it, was grateful for it all in one moment. He could not covet it though, only sit back in awe, like one watches a performer ... or lightning striking a tree.

"This is splendid here," she said. "This might be the first time I regret not being one of you people. Do all of you have gardens like this?"

"Most do, but most never use them. The expense of keeping them up is a status symbol."

"Ah, what a shame."

When had they become so close? Neither of them said a word. Ellie really was very small, wasn't she? She had to bend her head back to look up at him, but he couldn't think her a child. He looked in her eyes that knew so much more than him, and traced her lashes, and then her lips. Her lips were pink and soft, and she bit one a moment. Frederick's face was inches from hers and she waited. He wasn't sure of the look on her face either, but she did not move away.

"Shit!" Frederick got to his feet. "Oh, I'm so sorry, I ought not to ..."

"What? Swear? My father kept company with sailors. I have salty ears, I assure you."

She stood up next to him. Was that the flower's sweet smell still, or her? She was near him again. God, all he wanted to do was lean forward just another inch or two. The idea of it made his lips tingle. Ellie put her arms around his neck and pulled him to her.

Her kiss was soft, timid even. The surprise of that softened him even more. One hand crept to the small of her back and his

TO MASTER THE TIDES

lips parted, but it was not the frenzy of a night with a mistress. It was more like life-giving breath.

"Shit." He pushed her away again and paced in a tight circle. "I'm sorry, I ... shit ... sorry."

"Frederick," she said, "I shouldn't have come at you like that. You'll have to help me where propriety is concerned."

"I'm married!"

Frederick stalked off alone without looking back.

Damn. Fuck. Damn. What the hell am I doing? Ellie doesn't deserve to deal with my sorry hide. Isabella doesn't deserve it, either. He circled 'round to the beer tent and got a pint, sitting with it in a corner by himself. He could not see her again. They would forget him soon enough. He could always send Abby a gift on her birthday through the post. He wouldn't have to see them at all. No, no, no. He ought to break off all contact. But that wasn't fair. Ellie was refreshing. Ellie was good. Too good for him. He would write her a note to apologize and then be done.

"What are you brooding here for?" Margery sat down next to him. She had a glass of wine, one in a long line of many, from the look of it.

"I'm not brooding."

"You are. Did you go to look at that sorry Neptune statue again?"

"Poseidon. It's the Greek version."

"Oh? How can you tell?"

"I just can."

Margery didn't do so out loud, but she was laughing at him. He took another drink of his beer. He would not let her get in his head. Ellie broke that spell. He did not have to live the portrait Margery drew for him. She could say— "Be this!" But he did not have to be. Ah, Ellie. He ought not to think of her just now.

"Who was the woman?" asked Margery, eying Frederick over her wine glass.

"Who?"

"I saw you go into my garden with a woman. Who was she?"

"No one."

"Frederick, don't. I know you better than you know yourself. I can't stop you if you choose to replace me but don't do it in my own home. It's vulgar."

"I don't know what you mean."

"Don't you? Is she the one who healed your hand?"

Frederick didn't answer but his face must have been an open window. Margery got up and brought back a pint of the plain. When she returned, she handed it to Frederick. He refused. She dumped the glass in his lap.

"Thomas!" she called to a servant. "Remove this one. He's pissed himself and it isn't even teatime."

Thomas and another footman—both who recognized Frederick well—pulled him up by the armpits. Frederick shook them off.

"Fine, I'll go, I'll go."

"Your wife was looking for you," Margery said. "She's not feeling well and wants to go home."

"You could have said from the beginning," said Frederick, stomping off in a huff, the two footmen trailing behind, trying to look like an escort.

Thirteen

Frederick made good on his promise not to see Ellie. It wasn't hard when he stayed entirely at home or on his property. Cuthbert came by every now and then and Frederick resisted the urge to ask him about the incident at Margery's. He didn't mind about Cuthbert's fits anymore. The trick was not to let his own blood rise. The best moments were when he saw his brother flinch when Frederick stood up too quickly. Frederick had apologized for striking him that day, but Cuthbert wouldn't discuss the matter. It only made him surly for a moment and then he went on to the next "jolly" thing.

Cuthbert was at the club as usual when Frederick got there. The evening was early, but Cuthbert was already drunk as usual. He stood with Lord Fitton and Kilkenny, puffing on a cigar and blowing it in everyone's face.

"Freddy!" he yelled when he saw his brother. Yes, Cuthbert was very drunk indeed to call him that. "Freddy, come here! None of these men will have a go at pool with me. What say you? I've got 100 pounds burning a hole in my pocket, but I'd like to make it two."

Frederick joined them, lighting a cigarette to parry his brother's cigar. Frederick wondered if he looked that disheveled when he was drunk. The other two looked as rough as Cuthbert.

JOSEPHINE BORGIA

"I say I won't play him," said Kilkenny, wavering a bit as he stood. "Not for that twat wallop of a purse. If you all want to throw in for doubles, I'm in. Frederick here would make it proper numbers."

"Not fair," said Fitton. "This one is sober."

"Make him put in double."

"You don't mind, do you, Freddy?" said Cuthbert clapping Frederick on the shoulder.

Frederick shrugged. He was good at pool, drunk or sober, and he had nothing else to do. This would get his mind off Ellie, at any rate. Why did everything, everything, make him think of her?

"Don't have 200 quid on me," Frederick said. "What about all of you get me a drink and then I'll be ready to play on the level."

The men agreed and soon enough, Frederick was caught up to them. Cuthbert was way ahead, insisting on keeping his brother company. Frederick still shot a good game. Kilkenny paired off with him and held his own at first, hitting more slop than what he meant but as the others were too drunk to remember what he called, it didn't much matter.

Frederick and Kilkenny won the first round handily. Cuthbert said not a word but threw his pocket watch onto the table and racked the balls again. Frederick broke and the whole scenario happened again. Fitton, Frederick, and Kilkenny laid off the booze now. Cuthbert kept ordering. After he lost the second game, he took out a cigar, trying to light it with a wavering match.

TO MASTER THE TIDES

"Come now, man," Fitton said. "Keep the cherry away from the felt. No need to burn the thing down just because you're losing."

"I ain't losing," Cuthbert said. "Just behind." Cuthbert threw his silver-plated cigarette case onto the pile. Fitton hemmed and hawed but Frederick racked.

"He won't quit until he loses everything," said Frederick, managing another clean break.

The game went on. The three, less-drunk men got lazy with their shots, getting one in every now and again. At this point, they were willing to let Cuthbert win and endure his gloating. If they quit now, he would be prey to the sharks that lurked about the club pool room. Whetherton was already eying him from two tables down.

"Last game, wontcha say, Cuthy?" said Kilkenny. "I'm outta notes after this."

"What have you," Cuthbert said. "Don't piss about. Your shot."

Frederick watched his brother. Cuthbert had one eye open and wobbled where he stood. Frederick hoped he'd pass out soon, then they could divvy up the money and go about their business. He didn't care to drink any more. If he went home now, he would sober up just around dinner time. He could already feel the headache.

Frederick decided to end it. Cuthbert scratched on the cue ball when he was sizing up his shot and Frederick lined up a combo.

"Look at the little chit," Cuthbert said. "Thinks he can make that, does he? He always misses the rail shots. Just watch."

JOSEPHINE BORGIA

Frederick ignored his brother. Cuthbert always won growing up, not because he was better but because he always knew how to get in Frederick's head. He would prattle on about stupid things Frederick did or some such embarrassment until Frederick shook with rage and couldn't aim straight. Cuthbert was also a master at bumping the table so delicately that no one could be sure he did it. Frederick eyed in the line for the balls.

"Thirteen in the corner there."

"I hear," said Cuthbert, "that woman that sneaked into that beer tent on May Day has a heinous case of the clap."

Frederick felt his neck grow hot under his collar. He shot. The thirteen went in, so did the ten in the other corner.

"Nasty bitch," said Cuthbert. "Came right at my manhood if you must know."

Frederick bit his lip and called the eight ball.

"Told her I didn't want the clap! *The clap!* Did you hear me, Frederick? What was that woman's name? Mrs. Miller. Yes, Mrs. Miller has a nasty case of the *clap*!"

Frederick smacked his shot, the eight-ball fractured as it went in the pocket, and the cue ball sailed off the table. Frederick retrieved it while Cuthbert sang "Clap, clap, clap" over and over, laughing at his jolly good joke. Frederick went to Cuthbert, cue ball in hand, and cracked his brother in the skull with it.

"What the devil," said Cuthbert, dazed. He put his hand to his forehead, and it came back bloody.

"Shut your fat babyface, Cuthbert," said Frederick. He handed all the bets back to the men, sticking Cuthbert's ante in his pocket. "You're the only one amused by any of it."

TO MASTER THE TIDES

Frederick turned to go. Cuthbert picked up a cue and swung it at Frederick. He missed by a foot, but club men were all over him in an instant. Frederick kept walking, not looking back while his brother yelled.

"He swung first! Arrest the man!"

"Oi ya had it comin'," Kilkenny said.

Isabella questioned him when he got home but he said nothing. He was drunker than he realized. He went to his room, stripped down to his shirtsleeves, and fell face-first on the bed. All he thought about was Ellie. He could not escape her. She even slipped through the cracks at his club, that impregnable fortress of masculinity. What a joke. Her face was on his mind. Her kiss still tingled on his lips, the way she came at him ... Not like Margery came at him. Margery was possessive. He was her toy to play with as she pleased. Isabella always behaved as if it were a chore, yes even that night at the inn. Ellie came at him with pure joy—not even lust. It was simply a thing she had delighted in doing and could not help but do as the robin builds its nest every spring. Even the guilt he felt couldn't tarnish the memory, the feel of her small back in his bumbling hand. She fit perfectly there.

And he wasn't an entire fool. She kissed him. But now—he had embarrassed her. He would understand if she despised him. Best she forget him as soon as possible. If she only knew the things about him that he knew, all he had done in this world, how worthy he was not of this life. She saved him from *those* thoughts but perhaps he deserved those thoughts, the melancholy. She could be a demon sent to lay waste to the world by unleashing his foolishness and keeping him here. It was a Fae trick, to be sure. Frederick smiled to himself. He could not think ill of her. Never.

Frederick dreamed the fitful dreams of the intoxicated. He drove a cart with no horse that would go where it would no matter how he tried to steer it. He skidded around corners at ever-increasing speed until he woke with a start. He had dreams like that often. He assumed when he woke it was because his dream self didn't pull through. The bell rang to dress for dinner, but he sent his valet away when he came.

"Tell Mrs. Estibus I'm not feeling well. I'm going to stay in bed tonight."

It was close enough to true. His head ached something terrible. He put his head back down and slept some more. This time he dreamed of Ellie. She was going by in the cart this time, laying in it as if she were goods. Frederick ran up alongside, floating as fast as the cart. He was twice his normal size, big enough to lift Ellie out. The space around them changed and they were in the middle of a hedge maze. Frederick sat on the ground with her head cradled in his shoulder.

"I'm so glad you found me," she said, and pulled open his collar and kissed his chest. He held her tight, afraid he might crush her but at the same time knew he could never crush her. She clung to him, her tiny Fae fingers like vices, digging into his skin.

"Will you stay?" he asked.

"You must claim me. You must make me yours. Then I cannot leave you until you die."

"I don't want to mark you. You see I am marked." He held up his hand with an 'M' branded on it, black as the devil.

TO MASTER THE TIDES

"But I cleaned that," said Ellie, kissing the wound. The 'M' faded into nothing. "She is a powerful Leanan Sidhe. Take care about speaking her name. She can be conjured up at the slightest mention. Claim me, Frederick. All you have to do is claim me and you will bind the Fae spell."

Frederick sat up in bed. His curtains were still open, and the full moon shone bright in the window.

Frederick couldn't settle all the next day. He gave up on his books, couldn't sit still at meals. Even Isabella told him to get out of the house. He made her antsy, too. Frederick saddled a horse and rode into town.

The coffee shop was full today, but he managed to time it right to nab the table by the window just as someone else got up. As usual, he was the only gentleman in the place. He didn't care much. Maybe some other woman would catch his eye and drive *her* out. Thoughts of her were more intrusive these days than *those* thoughts used to be. They were both soothing in a way—*those* thoughts gave him an out, an answer to all the nagging horror that clouded over his days. These thoughts, *her*, were a balm to everything. No matter what he did, he always circled back to her.

The woman at the far table wore her hair the same as Ellie did that day on the beach. The smell on the breeze just now, piercing through the smell of horses and dirt. It was morning glories. Someone must have them in a planter. That was the smell in the garden. Ah, the garden. The kiss. It shouldn't have happened, but he would not give it back for the world. Why did he feel so guilty? He had been with Margery a handful of times since he was married and the Madame's house enough when the need was great, but why was Ellie so different? Ah.

JOSEPHINE BORGIA

It wasn't just need that drew him to her. The kiss was good because that was all it was. There was no hunger in her eyes, only glee. She loved the moment and took joy in it. He had, too. He did now.

Outside, a sound like a gunshot clapped down the street. A horse jumped and skidded a wagon filled with beets into the side of the curb. The poor farmer driving it clung to the rails to stay in the seat while the wagon tottered back to right side up. Frederick leaned forward to see down the street.

It was Whetherton. He sat atop one of those horseless contraptions, clutching the steering stick. He was wrapped up with a great coat and scarf up to his nose, wearing globe-like goggles and looking like something out of a Jules Verne novel. The thing puttered up the street firing smoke out the back every now and then. Horses pulling carriages fretted behind him, itching to pass. The street was wider just in front of the coffee shop and the carriage finally got round Whetherton, the driver cursing at him as the horses clopped by. It was a good thing, too. The horseless contraption ran afoul of a horse pile and stuck. Whetherton yanked at the control stick, cursing in his own right while the contraption backfired and puttered and finally died.

"Why do fools always have to make such a production of their foolishness?"

Margery came up out of nowhere. Frederick jumped in his seat spilling his coffee.

"May I join you?" she asked. "There is nowhere else to sit and it's silly for one person to hoard a table to himself."

TO MASTER THE TIDES

Frederick said nothing. She would sit no matter what he said. The two of them watched Whetherton for a bit. He got out and kicked the wheel of his contraption.

"Those things are all over London now," said Margery. "There's no getting rid of them."

"I don't understand," said Frederick. "They're worse than what we have now."

"The first iteration usually is."

Margery took a sip of coffee and watched him over her cup.

"Why are you here?" asked Frederick, still staring out the window.

"Speaking of fools," said Margery, ignoring his question. "I pieced together what happened at the party the other day, and Fitton had some interesting stories from the club."

"Are you talking of Cuthbert? His behavior is nothing new, though it's getting a little more public than I like."

"I'm talking about you."

"Oh, I'm the fool this time?"

"Yes," she said. "What is this newfound chivalry? It seems to be all directed towards a Mrs. Miller, was it? Really, Frederick, a tradesman's daughter? Even if she has money, you have to intrigue up or it isn't respectable. Not for a man at least. Women are given a little more leeway if they're older or their husband is a bore."

"I don't know what you mean," said Frederick, gripping his cup. "I've met Mrs. Miller, to be sure, but she is innocent of anything nasty you would put to her."

"Nasty?" Margery laughed and narrowed her eyes. "Neptune was watching for me. I know what happened in my own garden. Fitton told me what Cuthbert said at the club.

JOSEPHINE BORGIA

True or not, the county has been bored lately. It'll get round. She drew quite a bit of attention to herself on May Day. People wonder about her."

Frederick grumbled and looked back outside. Whetherton argued with a couple of bobbies. A couple more pushed at the contraption to try to get it off the street but with no luck.

There was nothing Frederick could say to remedy the rumors. It didn't matter. Ellie wouldn't care what was said about her. She was not in his circle, but he cared on her behalf. It was all Cuthbert throwing a tantrum.

"Don't besmirch the poor woman by pairing her off with me," Frederick said. "She's better than to take up your leavings."

"I wonder," Margery said. "I didn't believe it, of course, when I heard, but you've been different lately. You've never stood up to Cuthbert in your life. Now it's been twice in as many days. The only time you were anything like this before was when you first took up with me. Tell me, Frederick. What is she like? I know she can't be better than I was. Don't tell me there are real feelings."

"I don't know what you mean," Frederick said. "I've learned to push back against the tides, that's all."

"Now *I* don't know what you mean." But Margery looked serious. She wasn't teasing him anymore. "Has the melancholy finally driven you mad?"

"No." He didn't owe her any explanations, and she might very well think him mad if he told her. It was the shell bestowed on him by a fairy girl. It protected him from Cuthbert, from Margery. They were the two violent tides—one that flooded him and the other that stripped everything away, though he could never quite decide which was which. Still, Margery sat there and would not leave. He did not want her, regretted he kept going back. He would not go back. Not again. Not ever again.

Margery got nothing more out of him. He sat and sipped his coffee, staring at her, taking care to use the hand that was freed of her mark. She understood him, of course. She had taught him these methods of subtle jabs. Margery took a deep breath and put on a smile. If he had gotten to her, it didn't show.

"You'll excuse me, Frederick, but I spotted a friend of mine." She got up and joined a woman at the far table. They were all somehow connected to Margery. Women adored her. She was kind to them and allied with them if their husbands were cruel. Of course, the women would adore her. They listened to her word as gospel, too.

Frederick didn't watch her. He knew what was going on in the coffee shop. The whispering had begun. Ellie wouldn't care, he reminded himself, but it still turned his stomach. All she had to do was mention what Cuthbert said in the club. It didn't matter that even Cuthbert hadn't meant it to be believed when he uttered it. The rumor would spark speculation and birth other rumors and Mrs. Miller, Ellie, would not be able to show her face on the street. What would become of Abby? It wasn't fair.

Frederick watched poor Whetherton sobbing as a group of bobbies dismantled his contraption.

If that's your worst worry, thought Frederick, *you've got it better than most.*

Days went by. Frederick avoided society and even talking to Isabella much. She was wrapped up in every piece of gossip tenfold. She had nothing else to do. Her illness had passed, and she had a healthy appetite again, though Frederick thought her getting a little fat. He dared not say a word to her about it. She was sensitive about everything these days.

Frederick watched her today at the tea table. She was rather rosy, and he didn't think she looked bad plump, but still. Where had they gone wrong? It dawned on him that perhaps it wasn't either of their faults at all. They knew each other well enough after all the years and they got on but something fundamental was missing. A connection that would never meet between them. He had some sense that that connection did exist, and he was ever looking for it, had always been looking for it, like a key desperate to find its lock.

"Are you well, Frederick," asked Isabella. "Why do you stare at me so?"

"Did I? I'm sorry. Got lost in thought for a moment."

"It's well I have your attention," she said, putting down her teacup and straightening up. "There is something I wanted to talk to you about."

"Oh?"

"Pardon me, sir." A footman entered with the silver tray. "A letter has come."

Frederick took it and stared. It was from Ellie. There was no return address, but he knew the hand, like calligraphy from a hundred years ago. No one wrote like that anymore but for her, it was not out of place.

"Frederick?"

"Yes, I'm sorry." He stuffed the letter in his pocket. "Go on."

"Never mind," she said. "I see I've lost you. Go read your letter. I'll tell you later, but promise me you'll make time?"

TO MASTER THE TIDES

"Yes, of course," said Frederick, getting to his feet. "Of course, I will."

Frederick tried not to be hasty as he left the room and rushed up the stairs to his own.

Fourteen

Frederick,
I fear I breach protocol yet again by writing to you, but I wanted to apologize for the last time we met. I should have understood that you were not available. It wasn't very likely, was it? I am sorry to have imposed upon our friendship so, and I understand why you stay away. I do not hope for forgiveness, but I wish to extend the apology anyway.
Forever indebted,
Ellie Miller

Frederick hid in his room while he read the short note over and over. He did intend to stay away, but how could he, when this tiny bit of nothing meant everything. Ink on paper is all it was, yet the tide went out and the sun shone. What was Ellie to him? That wild animal he first touched in the moonlight. They were on the Fae side that night, two lumps of flesh, closer than any two humans ever were allowed to be. It was his first taste of the tide going out. Even during the day, the tide was there, pushing him to and fro never letting him get too close to anything. The moment anything became close to real, the current pushed it away again or pulled it under. That night, though, the moon came in and asserted her authority. One of her creatures needed him. The physician tried to push him out, but he fought back and wasn't having it.

TO MASTER THE TIDES

Now all of that was gone, gone, lost before it ever had a chance to flower. Sandcastles, that's all his moments ever were. That's why he despised novels so. People like Isabella thought those kinds of things, those kinds of romances, could happen. Poor Isabella. No wonder he disappointed her so. Those who wrote the novels knew, got a glimpse, and wrote what could have been. Their sorry souls couldn't deal with the loss so they created worlds they could control, move the tides as they would, to fulfill their wishes. None of that was real. One could never follow their wishes.

Frederick folded the letter and put it in his breast pocket, but then he thought better of it and went to his desk. He found the shell, still tucked in the pigeonhole. It seemed a brighter salmon if that were possible. He folded the letter as small as he could and put it in the shell. He didn't ask the shell for anything. He had no right, but he tucked it away as far back as he could and hoped that it would stay safe. From what, he couldn't say, but he wanted it to be there when he got back. Did he only have one more wish? Is that how the Fae worked?

It didn't matter. He could wish all he wanted, and it didn't matter. What mattered? Nothing. He tore through his closet, so many clothes he never wore, why did he have them all? He found his riding boot and pants and put them on. Never mind the jacket or the hat. He didn't care. Why would leaving off something so trivial shock people? He went downstairs. Isabella waited for him at the door to the parlor.

"Frederick, can we speak now?"

"Not now."

"Where are you going?"

He ignored her and went out the door.

JOSEPHINE BORGIA

He didn't wait for the stable boy to ready a horse. He could do that himself. He didn't know any of the horses anymore. There was one he took into town on occasion but that one wouldn't do. He wanted a good hard ride. Toward the back of the stables was a fussy stallion, mostly black with patches of white near his hooves and on his nose. Frederick stood before him and looked in his eyes while the horse pawed and whinnied. Lancelot was the horse's name.

"Yes, you're as cooped up as I am," he said. "How about a good run?"

The horse must have wanted the run badly. As antsy as he was, he waited patiently while Frederick dressed him.

Once through the tree-lined path, Frederick came to an open field followed by the rolling hills that led to the Fittons' property. He let Lancelot out just then and the stallion took off. Wind blew in Frederick's hair as he stood in the stirrups and bent low over the horse's neck, letting the beast run as he pleased. His muscles ached. It had been too long since he rode, but why? This was freedom. He had forgotten how much so.

Raindrops hit his cheeks, one, two, three, warm as a bath and he lifted his face to them. The deluge came down and soaked through his clothes, but it was hotter than the air and the horse ran on. What did he want? What did it matter? He rode on and on and on.

They came to a rivulet and Lancelot slowed down as he splashed across. They followed along the water for a bit until they came to a weeping willow. It was a place Frederick escaped to when he was younger, just on the edge of the Fittons' property. He tethered Lancelot to the tree with enough slack for the horse to drink his fill. The rain slowed. Frederick was soaked and muddy. He laid down in the wet grass below the tree. He loved the weeping willows. This tree's tendrils carried to the ground. You weren't hidden but you felt like you were. It was like he was behind the Fae veil.

His mother used to take him to this place when he was small. How had he forgotten that? They came there whenever he fought with Cuthbert, just the two of them. He remembered her now, hair just as fair and willowy as the tree leaves, eyes pale green. They went there and talked of whatever Frederick wanted to talk about. She never questioned him about why he and Cuthbert fought, and she never took Cuthbert to their spot. She never said so, but he knew she didn't. Cuthbert would have thought it foolish, weak. He would rather shoot with Father. Frederick never wanted to do that. He shot a partridge the first time he tried. He didn't kill it straight off and his father had one of the servants wring its neck. Frederick was 10. He held back his tears on the hunt, but his mother noticed when they got home. They took out the horses that day. It was the first time she showed him the willow. It rained that day, too, but not hard and they were safe under the tree.

"This is my special place, Frederick," she said. "I come here alone, but would you like to come too, sometimes?"

Ten-year-old Frederick laid his head on his mother's knee and cried.

"I don't want to kill any more birds or anything else."

"You don't have to."

They stayed a long while that day, even after he stopped crying and talked of trivial things. He remembered it now, the scent of morning glories on the air and the mist of rain around them, muffling out the rest of the world. They were behind the veil then. His mother could conjure the Fae veil. He knew that for certain now. How did she do it? Why had she not taught him? That was where the melancholy came from, losing that world, and he had it again with Ellie and her fairy daughter. He needed Ellie to fend off the monster that was himself and he pushed her away. In her eyes he was good. He was a man. To everyone else, he was a toy, a thing to be endured or used. But Ellie, as little as they knew one another, she saw someone worth knowing, and he could believe her. He had done something worth her respect. The night they met, her husband would have left her to die, but he stayed by her and brought a doctor. That was something, was it not?

Why could they not be friends? You cannot experience something behind the veil together and not remain friends. That wasn't even the proper word. Ellie knew he couldn't be anything else to him. She was a sensible woman, no sensible human being, more so than any other he knew, unselfish and kind and ... dear God, he was in love with her. This is what it was. This is what it should be and feel like. Real love only existed behind the veil and that was somewhere Isabella and Margery could never find. To get there, you had to care about someone more than yourself. His mother loved him enough to show him her secret refuge. Frederick risked reputation to stay with Ellie while she delivered. Now Ellie risked herself to apologize to him.

Apologize! She had done nothing wrong. Her kiss had been emotion, real feeling, even if it was only joy of the moment. Not like the stolen or manipulative kisses of the other women he knew. Even Isabella was only pleasing herself. Ellie ...

he didn't really know, did he? He longed for that heart-shaped face more than he ever longed for anything in this entire world. He wanted to show her the special place where he went behind the veil as a child. He wanted to touch the small of her back again and feel the tiny sure lips against his. He needed to see her now. She'd written to him, hadn't she? She couldn't despise him. He must answer her.

The rain had stopped now. Frederick untied Lancelot and dashed home. Up in the drive, Frederick reigned the horse in. It cantered in place. The horse panted but was not ready to go back to the stables. Frederick was not ready to go in, either. Isabella would want to talk but his mind was elsewhere. He couldn't listen properly, and he owed her at least that. He pulled the horse around and headed toward town.

People stared while he rode through. He had no hat and was in his shirtsleeves. He hadn't realized how covered in mud he was until people started whispering. How would Ellie take him? He looked like a vagrant. At least he wasn't drunk. Cuthbert had come home far worse before he was married, vomit all down the front of him, beaten to a pulp. Frederick was not nearly so bad.

He tied his horse at the stable not far from Ellie's flat and paid the boy a good deal more than he should have. The boy gave him an odd look, probably thought Frederick stole it, but he didn't care. He walked off, riding crop still in hand. He walked the streets, not paying attention to where he was going. The truth of the matter was, he wasn't sure he should go to her at all. Would she receive him? Did she despise him after all? Margery did things like that, pretend to forgive only to brand him or humiliate him later. No, Ellie wasn't like that. Ellie knew how to be an honest human spirit.

Frederick came to her building. The front door was not latched, and he went inside. He saw no neighbors as he climbed the stairs to the third floor. He had only been there once, but he remembered which rooms were hers. How could he forget? At the door, he knocked. Would the servant think him a beggar and turn him away?

The door opened and Ellie was on the other side.

"I'm sorry to come in all this state, but ..."

"Frederick!" Ellie laughed out loud. "State, indeed." She continued to laugh and then burst into tears.

Frederick did his best not to bungle the tea. Ellie's maid-of-all-work was off today. Ellie still had some of her dead husband's old clothes and loaned them to Frederick so as not to muddy her furniture. He cleaned up as best he could. The sleeves and the pants were a bit short on him, but he would not ruin her things. He brought the tea tray out with a cake or two and poured Ellie a cup, sitting next to her on the sofa. She had calmed herself now and broke off a piece of cake.

"These are my favorite," she said. "I'm glad you chose them." She sniffled a little still and Frederick offered her a handkerchief.

"What is the matter, Ellie?" he said. "I got your letter. Don't trouble yourself over me. There is nothing to forgive."

Ellie gave a pitiful laugh.

"I'm not crying because of that," she said, sipping her tea. She gripped her cup with both hands and kept it in her lap. "Or maybe I am. I don't know anymore. I missed my friend is all. I figured it was just like me to offend the one person who cares about me."

"Surely I'm not the only one," Frederick said.

"Oh, yes," she said. "I'm quite convinced you are, or were. I tell myself I don't care about society or any of that, and maybe I don't, but I should, if only for Abby's sake, and Stanway. I made such a mess of things, really."

"Don't cry," said Frederick, taking her small hand in his. It was warm from the teacup and his fingers were like ice still, but she wouldn't let it go. "Or rather, I shouldn't say such things. Cry if you want. Cry until all the poison is out. You may tell me what's wrong if you wish."

The flood opened. Ellie cried, unabashedly cried. Frederick pulled her close to him and let her cry on his shoulder. She was so small and shook as she sobbed, and he said not a word. And this woman did not seem weaker for it. How could she? Her feelings were honest and true, and she cried for her daughter and her brother. Not for herself.

"I'm sorry," she said, wiping her face with the handkerchief. Frederick handed her another, which she accepted. She sat back but he still had an arm tight around her and she laid her head on his shoulder. He leaned forward to stoke up the fire. The rain poured heavy again outside and it had turned chilly.

"Don't apologize," Frederick said. "Not to me." How could she ever wrong him? He could smell her hair. It was her, not the morning glories, that smelled sweet.

"But I do need to apologize. Someone saw us the day I kissed you. I can't bear to think of the trouble I caused you."

"Nonsense. My kind gets into that kind of trouble all the time."

JOSEPHINE BORGIA

"A woman came to see me. A Lady Fitton. Told me to stay away from you. You were hers."

Frederick tensed. "I don't want Margery."

"I know. I knew she was lying. At least now. There's a strain in a woman's eye when they are desperate for something. She had it. I'm not worried about her for myself, but someone spread rumors about you and I."

"It has to be my fault, Margery. My brother ..."

"I've been careless too, and I forget rumors don't only affect me. Abby's piano teacher gave notice. That's what made me realize. She didn't give a reason, but I know she teaches some of your brother's children. Stanway took it hard. He always does. He has high hopes of moving in the prominent circles, never mind that they won't ever have him. He doesn't have the birth or even the money to buy his way in. My father wanted to push him to earn it but that hasn't worked. He'd rather live like a pauper off me. I won't give him more than he needs or else he would drink it. This morning he heard the latest rumors. I'm to have the clap, did you know?"

Ellie laughed but Frederick gritted his teeth.

"Oh don't, Frederick. If I can't laugh about it, I shall surely lose my mind. My brother used it as an excuse to go on another jaunt. He got money out of me this time and I am afraid he will again. I sent Abby off to my cousin's with the maid and I am afraid Stanway will truly kill himself this time."

"Can I help in any way?" Frederick asked. Ellie was quiet now. His arm still was tight around her, and his other hand had found hers. They both stared at the fire.

TO MASTER THE TIDES

"You've done enough. Abby and I owe you our lives. The physician told me so. Had he come any later, we wouldn't have made it."

"We're even on that score," and Frederick told her about his original purpose that night.

"Oh, dear man," she said, turning to him. "Don't ever do that. Where would I be without you? Miller would have left me to die."

"I won't, Ellie," he said, and meant it, maybe for the first time. "Abby showed me the meaning of life that day, the way she fought so hard to keep her own. I won't say I haven't thought those thoughts since then, but I can't hold life so cheap any longer. Not with her in it and not with you."

"Don't ever, Frederick, promise me," she said, holding his face in her hands and looking him in the eye.

"I won't," and he meant it yet again. He could never lie to that heart-shaped face, cheeks flushed pink from the fire. What odd things crossed his mind just now, like how large his head felt with her tiny fingers on either cheek. How he wanted those fingers in his hair. Like she read his mind, they crept into his mane, combing the knots on either temple.

"You promise me, don't you?" she said. "No matter how bad things are, the tide always goes out again. You'll remember? You won't ever do it?"

"I won't."

"You promise?"

"I promise. I won't."

Frederick leaned down and kissed her. He couldn't help himself with her so near. It wasn't a hungry kiss, though his lips craved it. He didn't need to possess her, he only wanted to feel her warmth. Ellie drew closer to him, melting near bit by bit. She wrapped her arms around his neck, and he felt warm and safe for the first time in years. He wanted her to feel the same. He wanted her to understand. He tried to put it into his kisses, on her lips, on her neck, on her breast. She clutched his hair.

"Frederick, are you sure?"

Her breath was hot in his ear, and it sent a warm quiver down his spine.

"I'm sure about you," he said. "You're the only one who I can be my true self with. I hope you can be your true self with me. Don't ever apologize for impropriety. Not if it's your real feelings. Those are innocent and there is nothing to apologize for."

Ellie smiled up at him and pulled him down on top of her on the sofa, running her hands up his shirt, warm little fingers against his skin. He kissed her still and now *her* kisses were hungry.

Fifteen

Ellie washed Frederick's clothes for him and hung them in front of the fire to dry. Frederick did not go home, though. He stayed for supper and into the night and neither of them wore clothes for any of it. The moon was full again, as they lay in Ellie's bed with the curtains full open. Frederick wondered that the melancholy was gone and would he ever see it again. It was good to be happy or was he only borrowing hers?

Ellie lay on his shoulder, tracing figure eights on his chest with a finger. Frederick dared not move. She fit so perfectly there, he never wanted to get up. He ran his hands through her long hair, which curled around his fingers now that it was let loose of her topknot.

"I thought you were a Fae before I got to know you," said Frederick. She never looked more Fae now, pale face lit up to rival the moon.

"Oh? Well, you were right. I am. My brother and I are changelings, and Abby a fairy, born in the light of a full moon. I'll have to go back to them one day you know."

Frederick kissed her on her forehead and held her a little tighter. "I'll come with you."

"You can't." Ellie squeezed him back. "They won't take you unless you're full-blooded. You're only half."

JOSEPHINE BORGIA

"Half?"

"Your mother, of course. You revealed her when you said she kept the tides at bay. She had to go back to the Fae, you know. She didn't leave you because she wanted to, she was recalled."

"What if we did go away?" Ellie sat up to face him. She had her back to the window and her shadow masked her. He could not tell her reaction.

"What do you mean?"

"Divorce is so much easier now," he said. "I would have to play the scoundrel, leave Isabella everything, but she's not happy with me. It isn't fair to her to make her plod along. Don't worry. I'll keep enough of the money, so I won't be a burden."

"I'm not worried about the money," said Ellie. "I never cared about society but now it seems I do, all at once."

"We can go somewhere no one knows us. You and Abby can have my name if you want it. That will keep talk down. Stanway can come with us. I did a poor job keeping my own brother in check, but maybe I can be a good example for yours."

"You'll claim me, just like that," said Ellie, her face still in shadow. "You know nothing about me."

"I know you're kind, and honest with your feelings," said Frederick. "I'll always know where I stand with you and won't have to go about guessing if you're cross with me. That's enough for me now. We have our whole lives for you to tell me anything you want. Or is it that I'm not enough?"

He sat up and could see her expression now. She smiled ruefully.

"No, you're enough. You're everything." She held his face and kissed him. "When you're free, you'll claim me?"

TO MASTER THE TIDES

"I will."

They made love again and slept through until morning.

The front door of the flat banged open and someone crashed to the floor in the front room. Ellie slung on a dressing gown and headed to see what it was before Frederick could stop her. He threw on his shirt and followed, ready for anything. Out in the foyer, Ellie stood with her back to the closed front door. Stanway picked himself up off the floor, one foot at a time, steadying himself with a hand on the ground as he went. Ellie said nothing and watched him with narrow eyes. Frederick took it that this scenario happened often.

"Ellie, I need money," said Stanway, before he even was off the floor.

"You always ask, and I never give it to you," she said. "What makes you think today would be any different? Come to your room and sleep it off. You don't need to dice anymore today."

"They won't let me dice. Not until I pay them. They mean it this time. Who's this?" Stanway finally made it to his feet and laid eyes on Frederick.

"Never you mind," said Ellie. "Go lie down."

Stanway got up in Frederick's face. Frederick could smell the scotch on his breath. Frederick waited. He was used to this with Cuthbert. Best to let the drunk man rave until he was ready to pass out.

"You got any money? My sister won't give me any."

"I'm sorry, sir," said Frederick. "I've got nothing."

Stanway stumbled back a pace or two and eyed Frederick in his shirtsleeves with one bleary eye open. He laughed to himself.

"'Course you don't," he said. "You ain't got nothin' on. Ellie, you slut."

"Oh, shut it, Stanway," said Ellie and took his arm to lead him to his room. "We'll discuss this later."

Stanway shoved her off and Ellie stumbled a bit. Frederick reached to steady her, but Ellie shook her head. Stanway turned to her, glowering, but Ellie stood her ground, hands on hips. Stanway raised a hand and gave a weak swing at his sister's face, but she dodged and grabbed him by the back of the collar.

"Do you need help?" Frederick asked.

"No," she said, dragging Stanway down the hall. "He tries to act the big man, but he's too frail for that. One moment." Ellie put Stanway in his room and locked the door behind him. Loud thumps and crashes of furniture followed; Ellie came back to the parlor rubbing her temples.

"I'm sorry for that," she said.

"It's not your fault."

"It is, really," said Ellie turning back down the hall again. Frederick followed her until they got to the kitchen. "It's my father's fault for turning him mean and mine for not checking him now. I'm going to have to cut him loose eventually."

Ellie sat at the kitchen table. Her cigarette case was there. She pulled one out and offered the case to Frederick. They sat and smoked in silence for a moment, the curls of gray filling the air between them. Ellie gave a sad laugh.

"Are you sure you still wish to claim me?" she said. "Even if I do turn him out, he's sure to follow us."

Frederick waved the smoke away and took a good look at Ellie's heart-shaped face.

"Are you trying to get rid of me already?"

"Of course not," she said. She reached out and took his hand.

"We'll take him if we must," said Frederick. "Who does he owe money to?"

"Everyone all over the dodgy end of town. The card houses, the dicing men, even the Madame's house, I'm sure."

"No, they make you pay upfront," said Frederick, and then regretted speaking.

Ellie burst out laughing.

"Oh, Frederick, I'm glad you're an honest man. Don't ever change, but it is getting worrisome."

"It won't be long before they're at your doorstep if it's as bad as all that. Cuthbert does the same, but my father trickles in enough to keep his kneecaps intact."

"Do they truly break your kneecaps?"

"The dicing men do."

"Then we really must go and go soon."

"It will all be well, Ellie," said Frederick. "I'll make sure I get enough money, so we don't have to worry. Isabella will be more than pleased at what I leave her."

Ellie paused with her cigarette halfway to her mouth. She didn't look at Frederick but only smiled.

"You know, my first husband made a big production of claiming me but once he had me, regretted it. I'm like that, you know. In small doses, I do very well, but this, me all the time... I will always give you my opinion. You won't be able to rein me in.'"

"I'm counting on that," he said. "Why would I want to change what I fell in love with?"

"You love me?"

JOSEPHINE BORGIA

"I do."

Ellie laughed to herself again.

"He never said that to me. You know, I'm not sorry he's gone. I'm not. I feel guilty about it sometimes, but he wouldn't if the circumstances were reversed."

"I'm glad he's gone."

"I love you, too, Frederick."

Frederick went home first to dress properly before going to see Falcom the lawyer. He had to be handled very seriously to take on something so scandalous as a divorce. Frederick was willing to concede everything—the money, the property, admit adultery, and the fact he was unable to give her a child. All of that, no fault to her. He went over the terms again and again and again in his head while his valet brushed his jacket. He tried not to look around at the familiar walls. They seemed to close in on him, trying to bring him back to his old way of thinking. *Everything was pointless,* they told him. *There was no hope in his scheme,* but Ellie's scent was still all over him. He closed his eyes and let his hands remember the curve of her soft form. It sustained him.

Downstairs, he threw on his coat and ordered the carriage. He paced the foyer while he waited for it to come 'round. On his last turn, he saw Margery in the sitting room doorway. How long had she been there?

"There you are," she said. "Isabella tells me you've been absent for days on end. Where have you been?"

"Not days," he said. "I'll talk to my wife on my own, if you please."

TO MASTER THE TIDES

"I'm afraid she's asked me to be here," said Margery. "I think you ought to talk to your wife now. She's been trying to speak with you."

The carriage clattered up outside. Isabella came up behind Margery. Her face was mottled red. She had been crying a great deal. He had no choice but to follow them into the sitting room.

Frederick said nothing. Margery and Isabella lined up square on the couch in the sitting room to face him. Margery held one of Isabella's hands in both hers. He would tell them everything—he was going to eventually, anyway—but if they were to corner him like this, he would let them speak first.

"Is this how it is going to be?" asked Margery. "Are we to have another Cuthbert on our hands?"

"I'm not sure what you mean. I don't gamble."

"Staying out all night," said Margery. "Isabella told me. She's wanted to talk to you for a bit now, but you won't hear her. Did it ever occur to you it may be important?"

"I have something to say, too," he said, taking a chair across from them.

"I must go first," said Isabella. "It's only fair after making me wait."

"Get out, Margery," Frederick said. "I'm not a monster. I promise you I'll hear her out."

Isabella nodded and Margery left the room. Frederick tried not to watch her as she left. She had a habit of prowling about houses when she visited, though that mattered little now.

Isabella seemed to lose a little of her nerve after Margery left the room. She stared at the fire and opened her mouth several times, but no sound came out.

JOSEPHINE BORGIA

"Would you like a drink?" asked Frederick, getting up. "I know I'd like one."

"Yes, please."

He poured them both a brandy at the cabinet and sat next to Isabella on the couch. Guilt roiled in his stomach as he watched her sip her snifter. *Poor girl*, he thought. *She hadn't bargained for such a fool as me. I'm off following fairies and she did her best, really. I ought not to think about it. She'll be much happier once she's free of me. She can sell up if she wants. Father would be happy to buy and leave it to Cuthbert or one of his grandsons.* Frederick waited still, much more at ease now that Margery was gone.

"Frederick," said Isabella, straightening up where she sat. "I'm going to have a baby."

Frederick dropped his glass. It hit the rug under the sofa, bounced, and shattered across the parquet floor. Echoes sounded in his head as if things were crashing down all over the house.

"The night at the inn, of course," Frederick muttered to himself. "I thought ..."

"I thought so, too," Isabella said. "But isn't this wonderful? You said you wanted to start again."

"I'd given up," said Frederick. "I was going to let you be free. You could have the money, the property, all of it."

"I said I didn't want a divorce," she snapped, downing the last of the brandy in her glass. "You can't leave me like this. You can't."

"I'll take all the responsibility. No one will blame you."

Isabella screamed and threw her glass at the hearth. She put her head in her hands and sobbed.

TO MASTER THE TIDES

"You men are all alike! All alike. I thought you would stand by me, at least, Frederick."

"Isabella, I ... we can talk through this. Let's have another brandy and ..."

"Oh, get away from me!" She slapped at Frederick, but he dodged.

"Isabella ..."

"Get away, I said!"

Frederick did as he was told. He stopped in the foyer and told the servants to apologize to the carriage driver and the horses. The servants looked at him oddly, but he didn't care anymore. He was sorry as much to the horses as anyone else, being disturbed out of their comfortable pens— or perhaps they were looking forward to the exercise. Frederick trudged up the stairs back toward his room, untying his cravat as he went. He should have realized it was no use. Ellie was too good for someone like him and the idea of those thoughts was no longer a release. Well, why not disappoint her like he did everyone else? No. He promised her. A promise to a Fae was binding.

At the end of the hall, he paused. Had he left his bedroom door open before? He very well could have, or it could be a servant making up the fire, though it was too early for that. He remembered the crash he heard earlier, the one he thought only an echo, and picked up his pace along the corridor.

Margery stood in his room, in front of the fire, which did indeed have a good blaze going. The room was stuffy, like hell itself, and the orange light on Margery's face forced the impression still further. Bits of salmon shell were scattered about the floor, most of it ground to dust under Margery's boots. She held a couple of letters in her hand and smirked at Frederick when he came in the room.

"Only two letters?" said Margery. "We'd written dozens by now. You'll have to give her up, won't you? Don't worry. I know what to do with letters when you give someone up." Margery threw the papers on the fire.

Frederick didn't move. His blood rushed in his ears. He could hear it like the ocean in a storm, waves stacking high above his head. He tried to breathe but his chest was tight. He bent down and picked up one of the larger pieces of shell left, no bigger than a halfpence. The edge was sharp, and he cut himself on it. It bled but he didn't stay the wound. Margery paid his actions no mind.

"You should have stuck with me, Frederick, dear," she said, kissing him on the cheek. "You could have kept us both." She left the room, boots crunching in the debris, but Frederick didn't watch her leave. He put the bit of shell in his breast pocket and stared at his bloody finger, pulling the cut apart and letting it bleed on the rug.

Sixteen

Frederick lay on his bed, staring at the ceiling above. In his mind, the ocean rushed in around him. Cuthbert, Margery, his father, and now Isabella and the child added force to the waves. Before they were always content to push him about but now, they were swallowing him up. Ellie had been like the moon, pushing and pulling the tides as she pleased but even the moon has to set sometimes, and the tides always go in and out. They would drag him to sea this time and Frederick had never learned to swim.

The shell fragment was safe in his breast pocket still. He would keep it on him always. It was silly, but he saw it as a talisman. Margery knew it for what it was. That's why she broke it. She was one of Fae, but firmly on the human side of the veil. He was sure of that. She was bitter and cruel. He wished Isabella could see that. Margery only stood by her to make Frederick's life miserable. He would never go back to her. She saw that now and would never forgive him for it. He didn't like that Margery knew about Ellie or where she lived. Ellie would need to move soon.

But was he truly trapped? The plan was to be the villain in all of this. Anyone would condemn him. He was only trying to get around the damned patriarchal laws. Even now, women had to have extraordinary circumstances to take command of their own money. Ellie had. Her father had enough sense not to leave the money with her brother, but perhaps that was his affection for his fortune that caused him to do it, rather than a shirking of the old guard sensibilities. Still, there might be a way to be the villain in the eyes of everyone, yet not be still. He could have it both ways. The laws were sticky, but the more tightly worded one was, the more you could wiggle out the cracks between.

Frederick needed to clear his head. It rained out but that mattered little. He put on a heavier jacket, taking care to transfer the shell, and went downstairs to call the carriage again. He waited for it on the front step, getting drenched as a result. He didn't care. He would not risk Isabella cornering him again. The carriage rattled up in front of the house before long and he shivered as he got inside. He wanted a cup of coffee. The kitchen here hadn't quite mastered making it yet. He tapped the roof of the carriage and they moved on.

At the sweet shop, Frederick sat in his usual spot and looked desperately for the veil while he waited for his coffee. It was long torn down. Ladies sat everywhere, whispering more than usual and glancing at him. He ignored them. The coffee came. He took a hasty drink and burnt his lip and tongue. He watched outside, while the rain still fell. He shouldn't have gone out in this, the poor driver and horses. He'd wait until it stopped before he went back for them. It might be a while, but he would let them get good and warm.

He wished Ellie would walk by. If she were cold in the rain, he would have an excuse to go to her, but he didn't want to see her now. He didn't want to see her until he found a way to keep his promise. Out of all the times Isabella's news would have been welcome, she had to spring it just as he was near escaping. He forced another drink of coffee. He needed his mind to work, but it was as dull and foggy as the rain-soaked streets outside. He thought of the waves his mother always held at bay. How did she do it? With a smile and a wink of her pale green eyes. Abby had eyes like that. Where she got them, Frederick couldn't say. Miller had been dark from what he could tell, and so was Ellie. From the fairies themselves, he supposed.

The bell on the front door tinkled and Margery walked in like the bad penny she was. She was with Mrs. Whetherton, and they were both just as drowned as he was, but he couldn't feel sorry for them. Frederick looked away before they made eye contact, but she saw him. Mercifully, Margery and her companion took a seat on the other side of the room. Frederick sipped his coffee. He would stand his ground and they would not push him out. He wished he had an excuse to run out into the rain, but he had no Macintosh or gaiters, and he would be soaked all over again, no matter where he chose to go.

Mrs. Whetherton was going on as she usually did with Margery encouraging her all the while. Frederick didn't understand how Margery stood it. Whetherton was frightfully stupid, but Frederick hadn't realized how she went on and on. He tried to tune it out, but he couldn't.

"That woman, you know, the common one Cuthy had a run-in with at May Day," she said.

Frederick turned further toward the window, but he could feel Margery's glare boring into the back of his neck.

"I've heard some things about her," Whetherton went on. "Heard her husband isn't really dead. Too ashamed of the um..." her voice dropped to the tone of a whisper but still carried.

"...pox she gave him. Father was a sailor, so who knows what kinds of habits she picked up."

The rest of the coffee shop hushed. Frederick could imagine all eyes on the woman. Was everyone in there enough stupid enough to believe a stupid woman?

"Surely, you exaggerate," Margery said. She wasn't defending her. She knew what she was about.

"I swear I do not. Heard it from that piano teacher of Lucy's. If there is anyone reliable it's a piano teacher. They've got to play every day, you know, to get good enough to teach."

Frederick could take no more. He downed the last of his coffee and escaped out the door.

Frederick went to the club next. He wasn't sure why. It was the last place he wanted to be, but Margery couldn't come there, nor could any of the other gossips. It was always good for a glass of brandy as well and perhaps Kilkenny or Falcom would be there. It might be better to test the legal waters over billiards than come straight to their office. Was he still considering leaving? He wanted to play the rogue but not to Isabella's face. Not to her. Just the world but if he left ... There was no way out, was there?

He found his usual place in front of the fireplace, in the leather chair whose creases smelled forever of cigar. The philosophy book he left ages ago was still on a table. It smelled like someone spilled whiskey on it. Philosophy while drunk. That was a dangerous thought. One might come to any conclusion. Frederick ordered a scotch and leaned back in the chair with his eyes closed. He patted around his jacket for his cigarette case and opened it. It was full of neatly rolled cigarettes. It was all his tobacco, he could tell from the smell, but Ellie rerolled them all for him. When had she had time to do that? Or did she work some Fae spell? He put the case back in his pocket. He couldn't bear to smoke one. What if he never saw her again? He needed to write her directly when he got home.

The fire blazed up as a log broke and Frederick pulled his chair closer. He could not get warm. He hadn't been warm since he had spoken to Isabella. What could he do, really?

"Hiding out here, are you?" Cuthbert pulled up a chair, already half deep into a cigar. His tone was his normal jolly, but he scowled under his mutton chops. "Heard about the news from Lucy. Don't blame you, man. They get in a state when they're in that way. Lucy is like a mad cat the first few months. Didn't think you had it in you."

"Me, neither." Frederick slouched in his seat and didn't look at his brother. He wondered at his demeanor. If Cuthbert weren't rambling, Frederick would have thought he was in for a fit.

"When do you think it happened?" asked Cuthbert, twisting the cigar in his fingertips.

"That's an odd question."

"Just curious." Cuthbert bit his lip.

"At the inn, I suppose," Frederick said. He supposed that was the only place it could have been, but Cuthbert need not know that.

"Isn't it odd, after all this time?" Cuthbert said. "You were a devil to me that time, dragging me out of the Fittons'. We were having a jolly time. Jolly time, indeed. And you drug me away and played nice with your wife. Humpf."

JOSEPHINE BORGIA

So, Cuthbert was looking for a fit. Who knew what else he might bring up? Frederick didn't have patience for Cuthbert just now. He downed his scotch and got up without a word. Cuthbert blustered but Frederick was already to the door of the common room.

Outside, he shivered again. What was wrong with him? He was sweating under his coat but could not stop his teeth from chattering. What ought he to do next? He wanted to see Ellie. He should write her but that could go wrong so many ways. He would go see her now. The rain wasn't likely to let up soon and it may be too late if he waited to go. She would expect to hear from him after the last conversation they had. If he took too long to communicate, she'll think him a liar or a shameless rake. He couldn't bear that thought. He pushed on through the cold and wet until he came to the door of her building.

The front door was latched today. Frederick stood on the front stoop banging away, hoping someone would let him in. There was no awning, and it was getting colder by the minute. Finally, a ruddy-faced old woman with flyaway gray hair opened the door.

"Why don't you ring the bloody bell like a normal man!" she said. "Don't tell me you're here for that Stanway fellow. He's gone, and I've nothing to do with him, so you ain't getting no money out of me."

She started to close the door, but Frederick grabbed the handle. The woman kicked him in the shin and shut the door in his face. Frederick found the bell cord and pulled it. The door flew open again.

"Don't make go for my pistol this time," she said.

TO MASTER THE TIDES

"I'm not here for Stanway or money or anything like that," Frederick said.

"Oh? What do you want? It'll be a bit before the room is ready to let. They left in a hurry."

"You're the landlady?"

"Aye."

"Do you mean Ellie, I mean, Mrs. Miller, and her brother are gone?"

"Maybe." The old lady narrowed her eyes. "Who's asking?"

"Me," he said. "I mean, Frederick Estibus. That's me. Did she leave an address?"

"Frederick, is it?" She looked him up and down. "Yeah, you look as she said you would. C'mon. She didn't leave an address, but she left a note, for you in particular."

Frederick followed her inside, glad to be out of the rain and hear some news. He still shivered, even in the landlady's cozy parlor. It was a lot like her, decorated in the style of 20 years ago, with busy flowered wallpaper and dusty daguerreotypes all over the walls. She put him in the chintz armchair by the fire and tucked a blanket on his lap. He could see how Ellie would have doted on this woman.

"You look as she said you would," said the landlady. "Ellie said you'd likely show up in a state, and here you are, looking like you're at death's door." The landlady pushed a hot cup into his hands. It smelled of honey and lemon. "Lemons were a treat from the lady. She was always kind to me, that Mrs. Miller. Always paid her rent on time. Her brother was a nuisance but as he had nothing to do with the money, I let it be. I was sorry to see her and her little girl go. It was like having me own daughter around again." The landlady rummaged in a desk while she talked. Frederick was grateful for the hot drink but wished it had some whiskey in it. The woman found Ellie's note and handed it to Frederick. "You do look pale. Sit a while and read your note. Drink that down and I won't trouble you while you do."

Frederick laid the note in his lap and held the cup close. All the note had on it was his name, written in Ellie's swirling hand. It was like, what, miasma—Margery had used that word—it was a trail of magic, but to him, it meant more like a shadow of a presence. Ellie's writing was the miasma of her. It conjured the morning glory smell of her hair. He was afraid to read the letter. What if she knew what had happened and decided he was a scoundrel in the end? What if she realized she made a horrible mistake? Taking him on was, in fact, a horrible mistake but he hoped she didn't mind. He didn't want to know. At least she wrote him before she took off. Where had she gone? What if she didn't say in the letter? How would he let her know what had happened?

It might be better if he didn't. Not at first. Not until he could get it all sorted. There had to be a way to get it sorted. He finished his drink, warmed a little now; indeed, he was sweating more than he thought he should. He put the cup down and opened his letter.

Frederick,

I'm sorry to leave so suddenly. Please do not think this has anything to do with you or what we discussed. Please be assured that I remain faithful and wait for the day when you might be free to claim me. The trouble, I'm afraid, lies with Stanway. As it turns out, I am not quite ready to leave my brother to the loan sharks, so though it is his own fault, we flee.

TO MASTER THE TIDES

I must go collect Abby and my servant first. Then my cousin or my father's acquaintances may help us find a new place to settle. My brother owes a great deal of money to the Fitton woman's husband and he's pressing the matter. I won't give her the satisfaction of paying them. The money is mine, not Stanway's and they can't have it.

I shall send my address as soon as I have one. In the meantime, take care of yourself, Frederick. You forget to more often than I like.

Love always,
Ellie

Stanway. Why did brothers always foul things up? If it weren't for Cuthbert, he might have been free when Ellie came along. Why had Cuthbert been so insistent in the first place? But had he not gotten in the fight with Isabella, he would never be to Ellie what he is now. She might not have survived. She certainly believed she would not have. So, things could have gone no other way. He put the letter inside his cigarette case under the Fae-rolled cigarettes and tucked it all away deep in his pocket. He could write to her in Brighton. At least he knew where she was going. He would tell her everything. Every last little thing. She might disdain him after that, but he didn't think so. He had to go home. He'd send a man to town to post the letter. He didn't want to be out in the rain any longer.

He called his thanks to the landlady, who was sitting in the kitchen, waiting for him to finish up. She came out to bid him goodbye but instead rushed to his side. Frederick stumbled a bit as he tried to get up and get around her.

JOSEPHINE BORGIA

"You're white as a sheet!" she said. "Sit. Would you like a lie-down? I could let you into Mrs. Miller's old rooms. She's paid up through the month and all."

"No, I ought to get home," he said trying to get by again, but he fell back in the chair. Was he too hot or too cold now? He couldn't tell.

"No, no, no," she said, pouring him some more hot water from the kettle and stirring in some honey. "I'll call a carriage for you."

"Mine is parked at Blemmith Street. It isn't far."

"It is. You're not going anywhere. I'll send a boy to tell the driver to come 'round. You sit there and drink that."

Frederick didn't argue. He did feel wretched. He imagined it was the hole left by Ellie's departure. Just as well. It would give him time. He could sort everything by the time he saw her again ... everything.

He was behind the veil again. Ellie was there, her hair down, but there was a haze between them. *You should have claimed me, Frederick, made me your own from the beginning.* "But I couldn't. I was claimed myself." *No, you weren't. I cleaned that mark.* "Not her. My wife." *I was speaking of a claim of the spirit. It's too late now.*

Frederick woke with a start at the footman nudging his shoulder.

At home, even Isabella looked worried. He didn't wait to explain himself, only allowed the footman to help him upstairs. He did feel wretched. When he got to bed, no blanket was enough. He curled up tight in a ball under the piles of quilts. Isabella fretted over him and chewed her nails at his bedside, but he barely noticed her. He wished she wouldn't worry herself. Didn't she know she was better off without him? But he couldn't let himself slip away. He had promised Ellie.

Dreams and sleep came in fits. Ellie was prominent in them all. Sometimes he relived his moments with her. Sometimes she slipped through his fingers, like trying to hold tight to water. He tossed and turned and barely noticed the people in the room. People there were. Margery came once. He knew only because he smelled her jasmine. He didn't open his eyes enough to talk to her. She told him things, a long monologue of things, but he didn't hear any of them. Only wished she would go so he could go back to dreaming of Ellie. Dreams might be all he had now, all he would ever have.

If he were to die, he wanted to be in the midst of a dream of her. Maybe if his soul took refuge in the dream, he could stay in her dreams. He heard of the Fae coming to you but what about going to them? Ah, but he promised her he wouldn't die on purpose. He couldn't now. He couldn't. "Oberon," he pleaded in his next dream, "let her come to me while I sleep. I want her to know I'm keeping my word." And she was there, small and naked in his arms as she had been that day. *You are not keeping your word. You are marinating in your own self-pity and reek. Wake up, Frederick! If you are to keep your promise, you must wake up!*

Frederick awoke, coughing and choking on his phlegm. He looked around. His room was full of people and the sun shone bright in his face. His father and Cuthbert were there and Dr. Archer, and Lucy and Isabella. He blinked at everyone, trying to make sense of the situation.

"Where is she?" he mumbled.

"Here, man," said Dr. Archer, pushing Isabella forward.

JOSEPHINE BORGIA

Frederick took Isabella's outstretched hand, it was best to do so, and lay back on the pillow. They would forgive him if he didn't make a speech.

Seventeen

Frederick stayed in bed the next few days after his fever broke. The dreams of Ellie left him. He went to his desk several times to write her but couldn't find the words to put to paper. What if Isabella read it? Margery was her constant companion these days and would tell her to do so. Still, every time he thought of how to mask his words he felt more and more like a criminal. He would wait until everything was sorted. It had to get sorted.

He called for Falcom when he was finally able to get out of bed for more than an hour at a time. He received the lawyer in his bedroom with a hearty fire built up. No matter the heat of the day, he never could quite get warm. It was as if the fever took all his own heat and left him cold-blooded. He *felt* cold, knowing Ellie was so far away from him.

"What do you need me for, Estibus?" asked Falcom, taking a seat a little back from the fire. The old lawyer adjusted his collar. Frederick thought it better to make him sweat a little. He anticipated an argument.

"This whole fever episode," said Frederick, pouring himself some hot water and honey. Falcom turned down a cup. "Has made me realize I've made no provisions."

"You're young still, and strong," huffed Falcom.

"It's never too early, Falcom."

Falcom didn't argue. He pulled his lap desk out of his case and pulled out some paper and pen.

"I'll get it all down then get it typed up and we'll sign the official document."

"Very good. There's not much to get down. I want it all to go to Isabella and the child. Do everything possible to ensure Cuthbert gets nothing."

Falcom paused before he wrote anything.

"Is that wise, Estibus? Women are frightfully bad with money."

Frederick raised an eyebrow. Ellie was not. The housekeeper managed the budget here. Housekeepers all over the country would be out of work if what the lawyer said was true. Frederick didn't push the point.

"I want it settled on her just the same," said Frederick sipping his drink. "You would help her manage, wouldn't you, Falcom, if it came to that?"

"Yes, yes, of course," grumbled Falcom, jotting everything down.

"And Cuthbert gets nothing. I want that outlined in red if you can."

"That's not really the format ..."

"You know what I mean."

Falcom nodded.

"This is simple enough," he said. "I can have this drawn up in a day or so. Between you and I, I understand about your brother. Gotten worse in his ravings of late. Not sure what's come over the man."

TO MASTER THE TIDES

"Thank you, Falcom. Would you like one of these?" asked Frederick, motioning to the honey, lemons, and hot water on the table. "They're quite good with a tot as well."

"No, thank you. Is that all you need today?"

"Mind if I have one?"

"Of course not."

Frederick pulled a flask out of a drawer and made himself another hot drink with the whiskey. The solicitor fidgeted but Frederick would not dismiss him yet. He needed fortification before pressing ahead. He sipped his tot and let Falcom shift where he was.

"I do have another question, only hypothetical."

"Yes?"

"In theory, would it be possible to shift all the money and property to Isabella while I'm still alive?"

"I suppose. The courts will argue but it could be done."

"And make a small allowance for me?"

"What are you getting at?"

"Just hypothetical, Falcom. That's all. If I were to divorce, can I give her all my money? Make sure she's taken care of?"

Falcom scowled and shoved his paper and pen in the lap desk and wrestled to return it to his case.

"Don't ask me things like that," he said. "I wouldn't dream of bringing that kind of embarrassment on your family. Known your father for years ... Have me tossed out of the club, he would."

"Nonsense."

"It isn't!" Falcom stood before Frederick, red creeping up his neck from his collar. "It isn't right, Frederick, and you know it. You mean to condemn that girl and your own child? I assume you mean to take the blame, but she's forever associated. Do you not listen to rumors? You have to know what's being said about you but they're not all kind to her, either. She doesn't let on, but she knows what's being said. She's afraid for herself and no one can blame her."

"What's being said?" asked Frederick. He couldn't think of a single thing against Isabella. If anything, she stood by him when he didn't deserve it.

"Well, hmm, hum," sputtered Falcom. "If you don't know... Hmmm. Best not to feed the beast."

"What is being said, Falcom?"

But the solicitor hemmed and hawed and muttered about a good thing to have a proper will drawn up and hurried out the door.

Frederick should have known better than to ask Falcom. His thinking was older than the landlady's wallpaper. He and his father were two peas in a pod, and he would get no support from that quarter. He could not go to Isabella, either. Not until everything was sorted. Margery wouldn't disown her, so she would still have friends. Once he could present the possibilities, then he could go to Isabella. They would all see. This was really for the best.

It was still early, and Frederick decided to get dressed and go for a walk. The tot fortified him, and he felt better in spirit than he had for a while.

Down in the park, he looked for Ellie and Abby, though he knew they would not be there. How long had they stayed in Brighton? Were they still there? Was Stanway still causing trouble? There was too much to do in Brighton. Cuthbert had proved that. Maybe the foolish boy could run away. He was like Ellie's tide that went in and out on its own and pushed her along. She did her best to resist but she loved her brother despite her complaints. She would never leave him to it no matter what she said.

He sat on a bench in the park and stared at the people going by. The sun was out but it didn't warm him. He allowed himself to think of Ellie, how it would be when he saw her again, when they could be alone together, when they could go on holiday, and Abby could run on the beach as she did that one day. They might have children, their own little girl with a heart-shaped face, a boy who loved horses as much as him. *Imaginary children,* Frederick caught himself thinking, when he had a very real one on the way.

Ah, he was a horrible human being. How could he even think such things? He had to do something with himself. Something that made things better, rather than mope about and feel sorry for himself. That was his problem. He always waited for things to happen. He needed to start doing. Anything. Do anything. To the club again. He would find Lord Fitton.

As Frederick suspected, Fitton was playing billiards, shooting with Kilkenny. Friendly game. They played for low stakes and neither of them held the other to it much. Frederick joined them but only as an observer. He still wasn't feeling quite himself and in the dark of the billiards room, his head felt as if in a fishbowl.

"Are you sure you don't want to play, Estibus?" asked Fitton, as he scratched for the third time. "I say, you do look like the hell. This might be my only chance to beat you. We could get up a game of cutthroat if you want to take us both on."

"I'll sit out," Kilkenny said. "If I beat Fitton again, I'll clean him out. Don't care to win when I might never see the profits."

"Come now," Fitton said. "I've got deep pockets and you know it. Estibus, do you want to put a wager on it?"

"I do," said Frederick, racking the balls and lining up for the break. "You know Stanway Kenefick?"

"That one is into me for a good 3,000 pounds."

"That much?" said Frederick. More than he bargained for, but still. "No matter. If I win, you forgive it. If I lose, I'll pay it off. Deal?"

"Fine. I can spare it, really. It was Margery who told me to press it, after all."

"What's your interest in Stanway Kenefick?" asked Kilkenny, his eyes narrowed.

"Nothing particular," said Frederick, breaking hard and sinking a stripe. "Ten in the corner."

"I'd bet it's the sister," said Fitton. "Margery is a jealous one. Oh come, don't look at me like that, Estibus. As if I can't tell how she looks at you. Have at her for all I care, though I don't blame you for throwing her over for that Mrs. Miller."

"Sixteen side," Frederick said. "I don't know what you mean." He missed that shot. Fitton lined up at the two.

"There are rumors, of course," Fitton said. "I only believe half of them, but the way Margery is in such a rage every day, I would say some of them are true enough. I'd wager my townhouse it's the brother that has the clap, though. That poor bugger looks sorrier every day. Something wrong with him, more than just drink."

TO MASTER THE TIDES

Frederick frowned. He was glad Ellie wasn't around to hear any more of this. His head wasn't on right and he couldn't concentrate on the game. He made his next two shots but scratched on the third. Should have been a combo on the twelve in the corner but he bungled the shot. The eight and the cue ricocheted into the side pockets.

"Hah! 3,000 to me!" said Fitton. "No rush. I know you're good for it. You got what you want out of it. I'll leave the Kenefick bugger alone. Good hunting with the sister. Kilkenny, you'll excuse me, a man should quit while he's ahead."

Frederick and Kilkenny took seats in the common room. Frederick was still a bit weak to stand long. Kilkenny frowned at him when he ordered scotch but didn't stop him. Frederick wanted to be drunk. As drunk as Cuthbert on one of his raves. Frederick had saved Stanway from one of his creditors, but what of it? There were more and he couldn't go pay them all off without raising suspicion.

He and Kilkenny sat quiet for a while. Frederick was itching to ask him his opinion on the things Falcom wouldn't touch, but he couldn't find a way to bring it up. He drank down his liquor hoping he could get enough in him to blurt it out. After a time, Kilkenny sighed and ordered himself a brandy.

"It's really too early," he said, "but I might as well keep you company. You've got a bug up your arse lately, Estibus. You're turning into a regular Cuthy Jr. You want to tell me what's going on?"

"I do and I don't," said Frederick, laying his head back on the chair.

"Best to get it over, isn't it?"

JOSEPHINE BORGIA

Kilkenny was right, of course. Frederick took a deep breath and started from the beginning. The very beginning. How he never wanted to marry Isabella in the first place and his affair with Margery and how he met Ellie and even the Fae things. He told him about the time he spent with Ellie and his conversation with Falcom. By the look on Kilkenny's face, he was sorry he asked. He probably thought he was going to get some bawdy story and a fit of swearing about wives, but no. Frederick unburdened his soul. He felt as he used to when he read the philosophers but who knew if a man like Kilkenny cared for such things or felt that deeply. Frederick had some pity on the man and turned the conversation back to the legal matters.

"But what do you think of what I asked of Falcom?" he asked. "He's got some old hat moral qualms about it, but you're a progressive man, backed the suffragettes and all that. The old ways aren't going to matter in five years, 10 years. As long as she can eat, what does it matter if I'm around or not?"

"You're right as far as the law goes," said Kilkenny. He paused and took a long drink of his brandy. "Can I say this to you as a friend, Estibus?"

Frederick nodded.

"You're a shite, Frederick."

"That's the bloody point, isn't it? To be such a shite that the law is on her side. She gets everything. I only want enough to live on, and I don't care about living well."

"A child needs a father."

"What good are fathers? Look at Cuthbert. Look at my father. I want her to be able to remarry. She can pick the best possible father for her child."

TO MASTER THE TIDES

"You're abandoning your child, Frederick. You think that other woman will still love you after that?"

"Oh, God. I am a shite, aren't I?"

Frederick couldn't bear to go home. He took a room at the club and lay down on the bed, staring at the plaster ceiling. It was easier to find patterns in the plaster than think about real things, but even the swirls reminded him of the ocean. He closed his eyes and imagined lying in the sand while water swirled around him.

This wouldn't do. He needed to forget. Frederick got up and went to the toilet table. He splashed some water on his face from the ewer and looked in the mirror. Dark circles cut deep below his eyes and his face was pale. He should have stayed in bed a few more days. Or was it the strain or the drink? Or had he left part of his soul behind in that third-floor flat? He should get the landlady to let him in after all. Maybe he could retrieve it.

This was stupid. All for a woman who would be better off without him. Still, the emptiness in him bled and bled. How could he forget, let it go? Cuthbert always seemed to care little for those around him. His father went about his business without a care. Both of them spent most of their time at the club but that wasn't helping now. He could try the dodgy end of town. He had only been there before to search for Cuthbert when Lucy wanted him home. Frederick cleaned up as best he could and straightened out his clothes.

Out in the dodgy end, Frederick walked the dirty street with his collar up to hide his face. It wouldn't have mattered. Most of the men were drunk or keeping their heads down like him. In the street, there was a shadow of shame but the noises from the establishments were the opposite. Tinny piano music came from one public house and cheers from the dance hall. Frederick passed them all.

He kept walking until he got to the quieter end of the street and a rundown old building that had been there since the Restoration. It was a prestigious inn for hundreds of years but the family who owned it was ravaged during the polio epidemic 50 years ago. The whole quarter was. Now the inn was a brothel with an opium den in the basement.

"Up or down?" asked the rotund woman at the door. She had dyed-red hair the color of oranges and bright red lip stain that clashed with it as bad as oranges clash with chocolate. "Recommend up first if you want to do both."

Frederick nodded and followed the hostess up the stairs to the loft rooms. There on the balcony, girls waited for customers. Frederick chose the chesty one with peroxided hair. He didn't want anyone that reminded him of Ellie, but it backfired. The contrast was so sharp he couldn't help but compare.

Beatrice, the peroxided one, led him to a dirty little room in the back. It had one round window and a thick coat of perfume and face powder. It smelled like an elderly lady's room, which did not add to the mood. Beatrice turned up the gas lights in the room and took her fee.

"Do what you like to me," said Frederick, sitting on the bed. "I don't care what happens."

"Ain't about what I like," said Beatrice, "but if you think you're going to have trouble ..." She went to a table, the top covered with small bottles, most of them empty, and mixed some powder and water. The liquid turned to a rusty color and she handed it to Frederick. "Drink that down," she said. He complied, hoping it was poison. If she killed him off, he wouldn't be breaking his promise.

Beatrice left him alone for a moment, sitting in front of the mirror, humming "Camptown Races" and fluffing up her hair. Frederick lay back on the bed, wondering when the last time the bedding was changed. He was acutely aware of every fiber of it, every patch of dried something. What had been in the drink?

After a moment, he sensed his skin as if it were a separate entity. He touched his arm and tried to decide if it were his fingertips touching his arm or his arm touching his fingertips. Which half could he feel? The planked wood ceiling went in and out of focus. If he crossed his eyes and overlapped the image to two planks, they looked like they were coming right out at him. Beatrice came over to the side of the bed and pulled down his pants.

"Looks like you're ready," she said. He couldn't focus on her, only saw the haze of yellow hair and red lips. "Just lie back now. Let the tonic do its work."

He closed his eyes while the bed sank under Beatrice's weight. She held his arms above his head while she lowered herself onto him. The sensation tingled through his whole body as she moved on top of him. His head swirled and he felt like he was on a boat, bobbing to and fro. It was too much. He couldn't hold on.

"That's all you got?" Beatrice got up and pulled down her skirts. "Ah, you ain't used to the prick juice, I see. You sleep it off there. I'm gonna go get me a drink and if you want another go, I'll be back up in thirty."

JOSEPHINE BORGIA

Frederick did not want another go. His head swam and all he could feel was shame. He couldn't tell Ellie this. Or rather he could. That was the thing. He could go to her and confess everything, and she would understand, scold him for not taking care of himself. This wasn't enough. He wanted to forget. He pulled on his pants and shuffled out the door.

The rotund hostess at the front eyed him skeptically when he trudged up to her and said, "Down," but he pulled some money out of his pocket and she didn't argue. He leaned heavily on the wall while she took him down the uneven stone steps to the basement.

Downstairs looked like a cave. Uneven cracked stone made up the walls and jutted out at odd angles. The air was filled with smoke, and men lounged half-naked on cushions while Chinamen handed them tubes to inhale from. The hostess stopped by a sea-green couch and the man with the long braid nodded to him.

If this is another veil, thought Frederick, *it is not a Fae one. I will disappear here permanently.* He paid his money and took a long inhale of the pipe the man offered him. His head spun, and a warmth crept over his body. He lay there, he didn't know how long, inhaling when he was prompted and marveling at the feeling in his skin. It was akin to when he was with Ellie and he could never have that back now. It was gone, her warmth, her protection, the heart-shaped face all gone. The tingle of the drug was only a cruel joke.

There was no way out. He would go to Brighton and walk straight into the sea. The child that was coming had no use for him. What if the melancholy rubbed off? The poor little creature would be doomed with him before they even had a chance. He would say goodbye to Ellie and do it finally. But no. He had promised her. He promised her he would not. If that was to be his last promise to her, he would not break it. *Ellie, are you truly a good soul? Look at what you inflict on the world.*

Eighteen

Frederick awoke to his face pressed into cold stone and warm moisture soaking into his shirt. He tried but failed to open his swollen eyes and move away from the wet, but it followed him, and he grew wetter by the minute. He rubbed his face until he could get a good look around him. He lay on the floor and a dirty man stood over him, buttoning his fly. The smell of piss filled his nostrils.

"Oi, he's up!" yelled the dirty man, to laughter all around. "Ain't blubbering no more, neither. I get the five pence for waking 'im."

"He ain't getting up," said someone off to the side. "Lemme try."

Frederick rolled over into another puddle of pee and covered his head with his arms. He deserved this. After everything, this is where he should end up. He hoped he could die here on the floor and no one he knew would ever find him. It was not to be, however. The cell door clanked open, and a bobby rattled his nightstick on the bars.

"Get off him," growled the bobby. "Mind yer own business or I'll crack you one."

Another man came to stand over Frederick.

"Christ, Estibus," said the man. "Not even Cuthbert managed to get pissed on."

TO MASTER THE TIDES

Frederick peeked out from under his arm. It was Kilkenny, his fire-red hair shining bright in the light from the barred window.

"Leave me be," said Frederick. "I'll just expire here. I've already done my will."

Kilkenny rolled his eyes and motioned to the bobby.

"Help me get him up, will you?"

"I ain't touching him."

"Fine."

Kilkenny kicked Frederick in the arse until he decided to move. Grabbing him by a dry arm, Kilkenny dragged Frederick to his feet and out of the jail. Outside, he shoved him in a carriage, and off they rattled down the cobblestone street. Kilkenny sat in the opposite corner with a handkerchief over his mouth and nose. Frederick leaned his forehead against the cold glass of the window and tried to ignore the bouncing of the carriage. He wanted to vomit, and his mouth felt like he ate a fur coat.

"You stink, man," Kilkenny said.

"Isn't my fault," said Frederick.

"I think some of it is." Kilkenny cracked the window on his side. Cool air rushed in and he sighed. "You want to tell me what you're about? They said they found you in the gutter outside an opium den, sobbing. Looked like the den threw you out. Who's Ellie? Is that the Miller woman?"

"It figures I can't even throw a proper fit like a man. You should have left me there, Kilkenny. I'm no good to anyone."

Kilkenny regarded him for a moment with a sour expression. "They sent for Cuthbert first, you know. He wouldn't come claim you. Any idea why?"

JOSEPHINE BORGIA

"He's a twat?"

"Glad you're able to say it, finally. We'll get you home and cleaned up and then we have a good deal of things to discuss. I tried to come by yesterday evening, but you were nowhere to be found. I've been looking for you all morning."

"Whatever the deuce for?"

"We'll talk, I said. Just try not to vomit in the carriage."

Frederick kept his mouth shut. It was good advice.

He didn't see Isabella when he entered his home. Kilkenny took a seat in the morning room to wait. Frederick said he could come back tomorrow but the lawyer insisted on waiting. Up in his rooms, the servants drew Frederick a bath. He slunk down in the water, enjoying it despite himself. He watched his valet hesitate over the pile of clothes he left on the floor.

"What shall I do with these, sir?" he asked.

"Burn them if you like," said Frederick. He couldn't think of making some poor servant try to clean them. He scrubbed himself as best he could, finding sanctuary in the footed porcelain tub. If the tub would stay forever hot, he would stay forever in it. But it wouldn't and he would have to get out. What was he waiting for, anyway? He knew. He was waiting for the tide to come in, waiting for the forces of nature to push him this way and that, make his decision for him. He had never made a decision on his own in his life. Not one that mattered.

That wasn't true. When Archer told him to get out, he wouldn't. He stayed with Ellie and Abby was born. The entire worth of his life rested with that little family. He longed to be a part of it now. He wished he had stayed with her then. Her husband disappeared. He could have taken his place. Bah! What was he thinking? How ridiculous would that notion have been? He should have stayed a little. After the birth was over, the doctor really did throw him out to tend to Ellie. He didn't even know her name then. To Frederick, she was just "the woman." So many years went by when they were so close, and he never knew. So much time wasted and now, now.

He had to decide. Be the villain or be the good soul. Either way, he imagined he would be miserable. Ellie of course would handle the disappointment better than Isabella. She could take it in good grace, and how truly important was he to Ellie? Isabella didn't care for him, but she was in a circle where appearances mattered. Her husband leaving her just as she bore his child would be a social tragedy she might never recover from.

Frederick knew what he wanted to do and knew what he should do and the two did not meet. He wished he truly could be the villain. Cuthbert was on the daily and he still got on somehow. But no matter what he did, he stayed with his wife. That was how he got away with it. Father took care to quiet up the worst of his offenses. Lord Estibus would not do that for his younger son.

Kilkenny wanted to talk. Frederick would hear him. Perhaps he had more insight on what Frederick asked him about. More likely, he planned to scold him for the opium den. What possessed him to go there? It only made things worse. Even now, he could not summon one good feeling. The idea of walking straight into the ocean was more appealing than ever.

Frederick got out of the tub and dried himself off. He lay on his bed for a moment as he was, ignoring the goosebumps that sprang up all over. How long would Kilkenny wait? Could Frederick put it off until tomorrow? No. The solicitor was stubborn. Nothing to be done but go down. Frederick dressed, combed his hair, and went downstairs.

Frederick sat close to the fire and took the smoke Kilkenny offered him. He still couldn't bring himself to smoke the ones Ellie rolled for him. He planned on letting the solicitor do all the talking. If he wanted to tell him off, so be it. If he wanted Frederick to tell him what he was doing, well, he'd unburdened himself enough to the man already. Kilkenny could ask questions until he was blue in the face, but he would get nothing from Frederick.

Kilkenny waited for Frederick to finish his cigarette before he started.

"It was foolish of you to go on a bender like that," he began. "No matter how bad Cuthbert gets he's never ended up at the opium den. That shite will kill you, man."

"I won't be going back," Frederick said. "Are you going to rail at me for all my wrongs over the past few days, because I'm acutely familiar with them? Don't think I've been jaunting about, thinking this is nothing but jolly fun and everyone will love me better for it."

"I know, but that makes it worse. I don't understand why you insist on ruining yourself, one way or another. I know what you told me at the club, about the woman. That all passes. We all have one out there we wish could have been but give it time and you'll forget her. Don't be a complete arse, Frederick. You don't want to turn out like Cuthbert."

"I don't gamble."

"You think that's what makes him an arse?"

"The money, the fits. I would imagine there are other women."

TO MASTER THE TIDES

"You would imagine?" Kilkenny pressed his steepled fingers to his lips.

"It would be like him."

"You really don't listen to talk, do you? Sometimes you should. Even if you don't believe it, you can look into it."

"I don't care."

"I don't, either, but this time I looked into it."

That got Frederick's attention.

"What do you mean?"

"While I still recommend forgetting the Miller woman, I mean, c'mon man, you barely know her, but you may have an out with your wife."

Ah, leave it to Kilkenny—recovering Catholic that he was. If he had a chance to offend the church, he took it. Frederick should have known that he would come through. Damn what he said about Ellie, though. If Frederick had a chance to be free and clear, he would take it.

"Isabella!" A yell came from the foyer. It was a man. It couldn't be him. What did he want?

"Isabella!"

Frederick and Kilkenny got to their feet. The man was Cuthbert, in the foyer, struggling against two footmen, and screaming after Frederick's wife. Kilkenny went to Cuthbert and lifted him by the lapels. He tried to shove him back out the door, but Cuthbert's girth was too much for the lanky Irishman. They struggled and Cuthbert swung a pudgy fist into Kilkenny's jaw. Kilkenny stumbled back and Cuthbert broke free in the opening. He ran for the steps as fast as Cuthbert's fat ass would let him run and huffed it up. Frederick followed. It was no use trying to stop his brother in a fit, but he could make sure Cuthbert did little damage.

Frederick and Kilkenny followed Cuthbert up to the bedroom corridor. He was drunk, which wasn't at all surprising, but he stood at Isabella's bedroom door, pounding away and calling her name. Isabella didn't answer. Frederick wasn't sure if she was even in her room. He hadn't seen her for a whole day, though that was his own fault. Kilkenny tried to pull Cuthbert away, but Cuthbert rounded on him again. Frederick stepped in to help and the two succeeded in dragging Cuthbert back down the stairs. They got him to the sitting room and Frederick shoved a drink in his hands. Probably not wise, but it shut his brother up all the same.

"What are you doing?" asked Frederick. "Why are you screaming at my wife?"

Cuthbert's face turned sour. Frederick had seen his brother throw angry fits more times than he could count but now his face was twisted up like a demon's.

"Your wife, you say?" he yelled and got to his feet. "You don't pay any attention to her. You don't know how to treat a woman. That's why she came to me. Yes, to me, when she got tired of you. Now she's cut me loose and I don't know why. I did everything for her. Bought her things, kissed her properly. God knows I'm a better fuck than you; she told me so. God damn you, Frederick. I gave you the best prize in the world and you couldn't keep her happy."

"What are you saying?" asked Frederick. "You're raving."

"Damn right, I'm raving! Come at me, man! We'll settle this." Cuthbert threw his glass to the ground and put up his fists, though his aim didn't look too steady.

"Are you saying you and Isabella ... You don't seem her type."

"Is that what you convinced her?"

"Of course not. I didn't know anything."

"Cuthbert." Isabella appeared in the doorway. Her face was as puffy as the couch cushions. "Cuthbert, stop causing trouble."

Cuthbert's words caught in his throat. He went to Isabella and fell at her feet.

"Come back to me. I'll leave Lucy. I will. I'm sorry what I said about the child. We'll raise him together, we will."

"Cuthbert, I told you," said Isabella. "I wanted nothing to do with you after what you said in Brighton, and I want nothing to do with you now. You could have kept your silence and your dignity, but you and your brother have made a mess of things. I curse the day I met any of the Estibus men." Isabella raised his head with the toe of her boot. "Get out of my house, Cuthbert."

Kilkenny went to Cuthbert and hauled him to his feet. Isabella marched back upstairs. Frederick made a move to follow her but Kilkenny stopped him.

"Help me get this one out the door," he said. "It's better if he goes. I still want to talk to you. This is what I wanted to discuss, though I'm sorry you found out this way."

"You knew?"

"Only heard this morning, but I'll tell you all about it."

After they got Cuthbert stowed in a carriage, the two men went back to the sitting room. Frederick allowed himself one of Ellie's cigarettes and Kilkenny started on the tale.

Cuthbert had been sent for when Frederick was first hauled into jail. He was at the club as usual. He came to the jail but when he saw the state of Frederick, he left him there. He tried to come to Danforth. Isabella wouldn't receive him. It was too late and she was actually worried about Frederick. Margery was there and they succeeded in throwing out Cuthbert. He wandered the streets and ended at the club this morning. That was how Kilkenny found out about Frederick. He tried to send Cuthbert home, but he'd just got drunker and returned to Danforth.

The rumors about Cuthbert and Isabella had been around town for months. Kilkenny was surprised that Frederick hadn't heard, but no one knew for sure until Cuthbert went on one of his raves that morning. 'She's got to leave him now. No choice. No choice. I'll take care of her. Give her a villa in the south of France, I will. We'll raise our boy together and I'll leave him everything. None of my mewling brats now deserve any of it.'

"You see, Estibus," said Kilkenny. "This is what I wanted to tell you about. You've got an out, man. Leave them all behind. No one will blame you."

Frederick sat where he was without a word. He thought and thought. Could it really be cleared up so easily? Of course, it could not. Isabella. No wonder she had come at him at the inn. She probably already knew then. It had to seem like it could be his, but she was already feeling ill then. Frederick could only imagine the terrible things Cuthbert said to her when she told him. He was already horrible to his wife each time it happened though it was his fault. He should have left her alone if he didn't want children.

"Have you anything to say?" Kilkenny asked. "Shall I draw up the paperwork? I can tell Falcom to tear up the will you made."

TO MASTER THE TIDES

"No, don't do that," Frederick said. "I'd like to think a bit. I want to talk to Isabella first."

"However you please," Kilkenny said. "I can't understand you sometimes, Estibus."

After Kilkenny left, Frederick went up to Isabella's room and tapped on her door. She ignored him but didn't give up. After a while, she called out.

"What do you want? I won't talk to Cuthbert."

"He's gone. Tarred and feathered and ridden out on a rail."

Isabella cracked the door and peeked out.

"I only want to talk with you," he said. "May I come in or would you like to go downstairs?"

Isabella opened her door a little more and took a seat by the fireplace. Frederick pulled up the footstool and sat on that. He didn't want to be like Cuthbert, a towering maniac. He wanted ... he didn't know what he wanted.

"Will you tell me what happened?" he asked. "The truth. I am not angry. I don't blame you. I only want to know. I'll tell you all my truth as well if you want to hear it."

"You first."

He did. He told her all of it and held nothing back. He told her of how he met Ellie and his endless melancholy and what he suspected of the Fae and Margery and why he didn't like the idea of their friendship at first. He held nothing back and she listened. Isabella listened the whole time, nodding, understanding, wiping her eyes with a handkerchief every now and then but Frederick knew the tears weren't for him.

"There, you see," he said when he finished. "I can't fault you for a thing. I am an errant sinner myself."

JOSEPHINE BORGIA

"You think so?" she said. "I think you're just as human as the rest of us, bound and gagged by all the rules. I envy the Miller woman. She does as she pleases."

"Will you tell me what happened? Then maybe we can decide what we should do."

Isabella nodded. Cuthbert had come at her the first season she was out. They met in Bath. He was quite charming in the beginning, always flattering her and dominating her dance card whenever they ran into each other. Her mother asked about him and found out he was married to a distant cousin. "Cuthbert was all swagger," said Isabella. "Said he was merely looking out for his younger brother, still flattering my ego, telling me I was the perfect bride and were he 10 years younger ..." Isabella sighed and looked rueful. "He really knew what to say. He said all the things I wished others would say—and then, it feels so long ago, I thought his jealousy was a good thing. He loved me so much it made him mad with envy."

Soon after Isabella and Frederick were married, Cuthbert made his move. It was the night Frederick had seen Isabella in the hall. She was coming back from his room. After that, they planned many moments together. The night they were supposed to go to the theater, the separation had been planned. Margery helped them that time.

"I wondered why she helped," Isabella said. "Now I see she was trying to get at you. I thought she was just that good of a friend."

Isabella had learned after a time, that whenever Cuthbert yelled at Lucy among company, it was to cover his tracks with Isabella. Distract everyone with a tirade so people might forget he wasn't where he was supposed to be. In Brighton, though, he did the same to Isabella.

"I confronted him about another woman," she said. "I knew it was true, but you know how Cuthbert is. You could catch him in the act, and he would still swear up and down he didn't do it. It makes one second-guess oneself."

It was then she told him about the baby. He told her to get rid of it. He had enough damned brats and this wasn't the way to get him back. She didn't want to get rid of it, and now she was glad to see him for what he really was.

"I went back home with you after Brighton, hoping for a chance like we had at the inn. You were sweet to me, Frederick. I considered it, but how could I look you in the eye after everything?"

Cuthbert tried to get Isabella back. Nothing draws a spoiled man like denying him something, but she wouldn't have it.

"He started promising all the things I asked for, but I knew he would never follow through, not once I was in his grasp again. He was tired of me. I don't understand why he would not let me go."

Isabella wiped her eyes again and stared at the fire.

Nineteen

Frederick took the train to Brighton. He hated the train—the noise and smell of the burning coal—but it was the fastest way to travel. He couldn't drink on the train, either. The jarring of the cars on the tracks always made him feel ill. He was at his destination in a few hours, though it was not fast enough. He got Ellie's address finally from the landlady. She gave it once she knew Fitton had given up on the money though he hoped Fitton hadn't told her why. Frederick paid him in good faith and that was done. He had his father do what he could to call off the dicing men though his father didn't particularly care to do it.

"I don't even do as much for Cuthbert," Lord Estibus had said. "Men need to learn to handle their own debts."

"Has Cuthbert learned?" Frederick said. "And it's not for the boy. It's for who he will hurt if the dice men have their way."

"Fine. But I'm doing this for *you* since you never ask me for anything."

Ellie had her usual reprimand when Frederick showed up on her doorstep "in a state." How must he look? He hadn't slept last night. He could not help but rehash what Isabella told him. Now he had even deeper circles under his eyes from the drink, and insomnia, and the opium residuals that still made his blood feel sluggish. Ellie put him to bed immediately and sent her maid and Abby off to a seaside inn with a pile of money.

"Are you sure I'm no trouble," asked Frederick as Ellie sponged his forehead and made him drink his tea. "Will Stanway cause trouble again?"

A cloud passed over Ellie's face, but she smiled.

"Don't worry about him," she said. "He won't trouble us for now."

Ellie never asked him a thing about his situation; she only nursed him and fed him, and after a week during which he slept most of the time, his face was clear again. Once he was up and about, they took a picnic down to the beach. Ellie knew a private place, a cabin of her father's, that no one ever visited. They spread a blanket on the sand and ate their sandwiches. Ellie told him about her dreams of being a concert pianist, cut short by her stubby fingers. Frederick told her about his mother's weeping willow.

They spent the night at the cabin. Ellie kept it aired. She and Abby escaped there sometimes but that night was just for Frederick and Ellie. They slept very little. In the dark, Frederick finally told Ellie all that had happened. She sat up in bed with his head in her lap. He laid it all out, even the humiliating parts and all the things he had done wrong, all the ways he made a fool of himself and others had made a fool of him. He talked about Isabella and Ellie didn't stop him, only taking his hand and squeezing as hard as she could.

"Isabella's like I was," Frederick said. "I thought she was one of the tides, but she's been pushed around by them, too, and dashed against the shore."

Ellie said nothing but kissed him. Her kisses were feverish, and Frederick was in heaven. He lost himself in her body again that night.

The next day, Abby and the maid were back. Abby was over the moon to see Frederick and he took her to the park, just the two of them. Ellie managed to get her to leave Zeus behind and was able to wash him. That night they ate dinner at the table while Abby told about her day.

"Are you going to stay?" Abby asked Frederick. "Mother seems happier when you're here."

Frederick didn't answer. He and Ellie stayed up late into the night reading to each other by the fire. Frederick allowed himself one finger of brandy and the two of them retired together.

On the fourth morning, Frederick woke with the sun. Ellie lay next to him, soft breath touching his face so near hers. He brushed her hair back from her cheek and she woke. Ellie ran her fingers over his eyebrows and smiled.

"You have to go, don't you?" she said. "I knew this was too much to be true."

"You know I don't want to. Could you still love me if I stayed?"

"You wouldn't be Frederick if you abandoned her."

"You think I'm that noble?"

"Don't argue with me, Frederick. I don't like it."

Frederick laughed and pulled her close one more time.

On the train home, Frederick thought about his last moments with Ellie. They kissed on her doorstep, not caring who saw. He broke down for a moment, begged her to let him stay. He could be good to her. He could leave Isabella all the money in the world if only Ellie would have him.

"Frederick, you said yourself, Isabella was a victim of the tides. You wanted to master the tides. Do you remember? But once you do, you have a responsibility to those they push about. I think you know this in your heart. Of course, I want you to stay but could you live with yourself if you did?"

Frederick only kissed her more.

"Be a gentle master, Frederick, and remember your promise to me," she said. "You promised me you would care for yourself."

"I will, Ellie. Even when I don't want to."

The train shook and bounced all the way back to the station near his home. He allowed himself to think of Ellie the whole way, every curve of her body, every soft warm crevasse, the smell of her morning glory hair, and the line his finger traced around her heart-shaped face. How could she do that? How could she make him feel so whole even when he came to her as such a fool? She accepted him for all of it and that is why he could tell her everything.

Back at home, he found Isabella in her room sitting in a chair by the window. Her embroidery was abandoned in her lap. Her face was blank, but there were no tear stains on her cheeks. She wasn't aware of him right away and she reached up and rubbed her belly. A sad smile turned up one corner of her mouth.

"Isabella," Frederick said. She nearly jumped out of her seat.

"Oh!" she said. "You're back. I ... I'm sorry. I'm glad you're back, actually." She was flustered and didn't know what to say.

"How are you feeling today?" he asked.

"Well enough."

JOSEPHINE BORGIA

"Will you come with me? I want to show you something."

Frederick took her to the stables first. The little butter horse was still there, as gentle as ever. She nuzzled Isabella and Isabella patted her nose. Once seated they set out across the land. It was a beautiful day. Isabella looked frightened, however, but Frederick wouldn't speak until he could explain himself. They got to the weeping willow and Frederick helped Isabella off the horse. He spread a blanket down under the tree and asked her to sit.

"My mother used to take me here when things were difficult, he said. "I thought we could sit and talk awhile."

"Are you leaving me, Frederick?"

"No, unless that's what you want."

Isabella drew her knees to her chest. Frederick could see her shaking but she did not cry. She reached out with her hand and laid it on his arm, squeezing tight.

"I know what Cuthbert is," he said. "I know how he works. I'm glad you're shut of him. And now we know the problem of children lies with me. I know you wanted children. If you want me to stay, I'll raise the child as if they're mine. Let all the gossips wonder."

"What of Ellie, the woman you told me about? Did she not love you?"

"She did. And I loved her."

"Then why are you here with me?" The tears came now, and Isabella hid her face in her knees.

"I can't leave you to them. It's their fault you have the life you do. I've been pushed around by them all my life, but no more. I will stay and fend off Cuthbert and Margery and whoever else. I know you don't love me, and you know where my heart is, but we could be friends, companions. I'll fight them all off for you if only to not let the tides drown anyone else, not in my world. Not ever again."

"Yes, that's exactly how they are, isn't it? Dragging you down with their undertow no matter how you fight or protest. The whole while I convinced myself I loved Cuthbert, I secretly hated him. I hated him for making me into the type of woman who keeps secrets. I hated him for making me lie. The night at the inn. Frederick, I'm so sorry; you seemed so hopeful, so I drank and drank to keep myself playing along, and then you seemed so hurt I almost kept up the pretense for your sake. I know you tried with me. I did in the beginning. I promise I did. I'll try now."

"Only be honest with me and yourself. That's all I'm asking of myself, at any rate. If we can give this child a taste of a happy home, then we've done more than most parents."

Isabella and Frederick spent the rest of the afternoon under the tree. Isabella did try; she asked Frederick about his books and promised to read one someday, but he said don't bother. The old philosophies don't stand any more. They ought to find new books together.

"Can I meet Ellie one day?" asked Isabella "She sounds like the kind of woman I want to be, but for now, I need to lean on you. She probably hates me, though."

"I doubt she does. She understands the world and sees it for what it is. I don't think I could meet her again."

The two went back, Isabella again riding the little butter horse, and Frederick spent the rest of the day in his room.

Some days later, Frederick showed Isabella his coffee shop. It was full of ladies, Margery and Mrs. Whetherton among them. Frederick walked in with Isabella on his arm. The tinkle of the bell attached to the door was like a thunderclap that silenced the talk in the room. Isabella shrunk back but Frederick patted her hand.

"You really must try their biscuits," he said. "They're very good. I like this table over here away from all the old biddies." He didn't care who heard him. A "tsk" or two came from the group but he ignored it. Frederick helped Isabella up onto the high stool.

"Never mind all them," said Frederick. "If we ignore them long enough, they'll get bored. I really do come here for the biscuits and there's a nice view of the street to watch people pass by."

Isabella was still tense, but she focused on the scene outside. Frederick watched the ladies in the room, eying each one in turn. One by one, they turned back to their neighbors and took up whispering again. Margery still watched them. Frederick stared back, sipping his coffee, and watching her over his cup. His ears rang with the sound of the ocean, but he imagined himself a high cliff. The tide rolled in but broke against the side of him. Over and over the water battered the rocks but the rocks stood.

Margery snorted and excused herself. She didn't look at Frederick or Isabella when she went out the door. Isabella watched her the entire way down the street.

"Have you given thought to names?" Frederick asked.

"What? Oh," Isabella stirred more cream in her tea. "I have. Henry, if it's a boy. Charlotte, if it's a girl."

"You seem pretty sure."

TO MASTER THE TIDES

"They were my grandparents on my mother's side. They were always very sweet to me when I was small."

"Then, they are good names."

Frederick snickered to himself at the confusion on Mrs. Whetherton's face. He brought up the book he and Isabella were reading. Once engaged, Isabella did have a good understanding of the things she read. She was merely out of practice from the company she normally kept. Frederick listened to her talk. She brought a whole new perspective to things, different from his or even Ellie's. It was bright and optimistic; Frederick marveled that she still had that view, after everything. Cuthbert couldn't ruin her as he had so many around him.

Cuthbert did try to come back time and again. He wouldn't leave them alone. He wrote to Isabella and banged on the door at all hours of the night. Isabella burned all his letters without reading them and the servants were instructed to use all means of force necessary to keep Cuthbert out. Lucy was too embarrassed to show her face. She took their myriad of children off to her mother's and stayed there. Lord Estibus had enough as well. Still strong for his age, he gave Cuthbert a good wallop and left for the townhouse. That left Cuthbert to the loan sharks, so he couldn't leave the house. Frederick and Isabella were finally left in peace.

A month later, Cuthbert disappeared. The servants couldn't say where he went or when he got out. Only that a horse was missing from the stables. Lucy and Lord Estibus came home, Lucy leaving the children with their mother. Still, Cuthbert didn't turn up. The police searched all the houses up and down the dodgy end of town. Even the dicing men hadn't seen him.

Frederick didn't worry at first. Cuthbert disappeared on the regular, but after a week or so, he still didn't turn up. The police pressed the dicing men harder, but they only confessed that he still owed them and if anyone knew where he was, they would be much obliged.

Lord Estibus hired a private investigator, but they turned up nothing. Lucy kept to herself. Frederick saw her every now and then. Isabella visited, too, though Lucy didn't have any words for her. It was too hard for Isabella, too, as her stomach grew. Frederick considered leaving the county, but he had to know what had become of his brother, for better or worse.

After no word for several more months, Frederick got a note from an address in Surrey. The hand was that of a woman but no one he recognized, and the note smelled of perfume and cigar. All the note said was to come to the address as soon as ever possible.

Frederick had to go. He took the awful train again. If he had to take the train, he would rather be going south to Brighton instead of north to Surrey. The train made him think of Ellie. He still had the cigarettes she rolled, too stale to be smoked now, but he carried them in his pocket. Her last letter was still tucked under them. He had so few things from her. On the train he let himself imagine that he was going back again to stay. Only on the train would he allow himself to recapture the moments he had with her.

Once in Surrey, he went straight to the address from the letter. It was in an older part of town. The gray house was stuffed between two others on a narrow road. All the homes had rotting wood shutters and dirty windows and seemed unbearably damp despite the dry sunny day. A baby cried in the house next door and a flea-ridden mongrel scratched an ear on the porch.

Frederick rang the bell. A thin woman, about 20, with painted lips and her hair bound up in a scarf, answered the door. She didn't say anything, only looked Frederick up and down. He held up the letter he had and tried to explain himself. The woman's eyes landed on it for a moment, and she nodded.

"Come," said the woman, turning to go in the house.

Frederick followed her. The house smelled of cat pee and creaked wherever he walked. He followed the woman up the rickety steps.

"You may be in time," she said, "or you may not. I haven't checked this morning."

The woman took him to a room at the end of the hall and motioned towards it. She would not go in herself. Frederick opened the door and the smell of shit and rotting flesh about knocked him down. Cuthbert lay in the bed, still breathing, but a skeleton of what he once was, his fat baby cheeks deflated and drawn about his skull. He turned a bleary eye toward Frederick and attempted a smile.

Frederick went to the bed and lifted the blanket. Cuthbert's legs were mangled and bruised. Wounds pussed green all over them and the flesh was dead in places. Gangrene snaked up his veins.

"What happened?" asked Frederick, putting a handkerchief to his mouth and nose. "Who does he owe?"

JOSEPHINE BORGIA

"Did it to himself," the woman said from outside the door. "Tripped one night while he was drunk. Fell down some stairs. Legs got all twisted up and he fell on top of them."

"Didn't you call a surgeon?"

"Tried but he wouldn't come to this end of town until he finished with all his paying patients. It was two weeks before they saw him and by then the rot set in. Said they'd have to take the legs off but Cuthy here refused to let them."

"There must be something they can do for him," Frederick said.

"No. Too late now."

Frederick knelt near the bed and took his brother's hand.

"Cuthbert, can you hear me?"

Cuthbert turned and nodded.

"Is there anything you want?" asked Frederick. "Anything I can do for you?"

Cuthbert shook his head.

"I'll come right back, brother," Frederick said.

In town, Frederick had no idea where he was going but soon got directions. He stopped at the drug store and bought as much laudanum as they would allow. He went to the tobacconist's shop and bought a box of Partagàs. He went to the liquor store and bought a bottle of scotch. Next, he went to the bookstore and found "The Prisoner of Zenda." He came back to the Surrey house, arms full. He didn't wait to be invited in, though the woman was clearly surprised to see him back.

"Could you bring some glasses?" he said, heading up the stairs. "One for yourself if you like scotch."

The woman joined them in the room soon after Frederick got there. He opened a window, though the smell wasn't much better from the alley. Still, the air lifted some of the staleness from the room. The woman left after she got her scotch. Cuthbert watched them all but didn't say a thing.

"Can you sit?" Frederick asked. Cuthbert nodded but, in the end, Frederick had to sit him up. Cuthbert winced but said nothing. Frederick lined up the bottles of laudanum on the side table and Cuthbert reached for one. "Easy," Frederick said, "those have to last you." Cuthbert grumbled and took a swig. He seemed to relax a little as the drug took effect. Frederick took out the box of cigars, lighting one. He put a dirty plate on Cuthbert's lap to use as an ashtray and stuck the cigar in Cuthbert's mouth. The sick man took a few puffs, blowing the smoke out his nose and coughing a little. A hint of a smile crooked the corner of his mouth. Frederick sat back in the dirty armchair and pulled out the book.

"Isabella was reading this one," Frederick said. Cuthbert started but could say nothing. Frederick took the cigar from him and ashed it on the plate. He went to stick it back in Cuthbert's mouth but Cuthy managed to take it himself. He took another drink of laudanum and nodded at the book. Frederick read to him until he fell asleep. He rolled the cigar in the plate and let Cuthbert be for a time.

Frederick stayed for the next four days, finishing the book on the third.

Cuthbert expired just before the laudanum ran out.

Twenty

Just after the baby, a boy they did name Henry, was born, Frederick and Isabella sold Danforth. Every last bit of it, down to the furniture and the horses. They took only their clothes and books and the few servants who wished to remain with them.

Frederick put the estate up at auction. His father wanted it, of course, but he made such an insulting offer, Frederick would not take it. He wasn't desperate to leave. He could sit until he got the money he wanted. Frederick sat in the back of the auction house as the price went up and up. As Frederick presumed, Lord Estibus got it in the end, but he was obliged to pay half again what it was worth. The money was enough for Frederick and Isabella to live on for the rest of their lives and still leave a bit for Henry.

Once the sale was complete, they moved far to the north, up near Newcastle. The old Roman wall was still there in places and Frederick had always wanted to see it. They bought a small house in town; cozy, Isabella called it. Frederick left their new address in the hands of Kilkenny and asked him to handle all correspondence. No one wrote. Their old community forgot them as soon as they were gone, or likely didn't, using them as fodder for talk now that they weren't there to defend themselves.

TO MASTER THE TIDES

Frederick got only one letter six months after they moved. His father had finally died. Everything—including Lord Estibus' estate and Danforth—was left to Cuthbert's eldest son Thomas, who was 12. Kilkenny and the estate steward would manage it for him, and Lucy was assured a place for life. The boy was still young and Kilkenny knew the family well. Frederick was glad Thomas would have him as an example instead of his father. He'd inherited Cuthbert's cheeks but his mother's timidity. The brash Irishman would do him good.

Small provisions were made for each of the grandchildren, including Henry, who was of Estibus blood after all, even if his origins were ignoble. It was a good sum of 5,000 pounds, to be paid out on his 18th birthday. The provisions were put in place while Cuthbert was alive, and Lord Estibus had not changed his will.

"I suppose we couldn't hope for much," Frederick said when Isabella had finished reading Kilkenny's letter about Lord Estibus' estate. The two sat on the terrace of their tidy Newcastle home. They had a small shotgun garden extending to the carriage house. Little Henry played on a blanket in the grass.

"But we don't need it, do we?" she said. "I'm glad Henry wasn't forgotten."

"He is an Estibus, after all, one way or another. Father put too much stock in blood to ignore him."

Isabella watched the boy rock on his knees, intent on grabbing a blade of grass.

"I hope he doesn't turn out like Cuthbert," she said. "I worry for him."

"Father was too strict with Cuthbert, and Cuthy couldn't get past our mother's death. That's when he changed. He was good and honest when we were boys, always protected his shy little brother."

"And you," Isabella said. "Is that when the melancholy came on?"

"No," he said. "I think I've always been this way. Mother always knew what to do about it though."

Isabella made herself a happy life. Though she never would be accepted into the upper circles of society, she and Frederick were the most prominent among the middle class. Those who knew Isabella liked her. She got drawn into politics, of all things, and joined the suffragette movement along with some of her friends. Still a bit spoiled and entitled, she was a formidable adversary to those who tried to shout her down. Frederick encouraged it, was proud of her even, and sorry he didn't see as much in her when they first met. He told her as much the day she came back from her first protest. Her hair was pulled out of her chignon and, she had a black eye from a run-in with a bobby. She gave as good as she got though, wrestling the nightstick from the man's hand. Frederick was fortunate enough to have enough banknotes on him to bribe her out of jail.

Isabella paced their parlor, retelling the whole scene.

"And then, Martha whopped the bobby with her sign. Oh, it was glorious. He came at us in his little prick helmet, oops, sorry, that's what Martha calls them."

"Go on, go on."

"Well, he comes at us, and that's when the fighting broke out, but the fool didn't know what he was about in all that riot.

Used to bullying drunks and all that. That's all they're good for anyway, you know. Starts calling us all sorts of names, and then I got separated in the shoving." Isabella fell into a chair next to Frederick's. He handed her a glass of wine that she gratefully took. "Thank you for coming to get me out of jail."

Frederick shrugged.

"Of course, I'd come get you. What are they about, locking up women?"

"Don't be like that. If we expect to be treated equally, it must be for everything. Even the bad parts. I'll take the bad with the good."

"I am proud of you," said Frederick. "You've grown a great deal when left to your own devices."

"Have I? Am I so different?"

"Not different. The optimism is still there, but you've broken free of the noose of the set's way of thinking."

"I don't know about that," she said. "I do know I'm glad you don't tell me how to be and what to think. My parents did. Cuthbert did. Even Margery. I remember once, with Cuthbert, when I still believed I loved him, I ventured my own opinion on something. I said, 'Isn't it silly that women aren't allowed the vote? They know just as much about the world as the men do.' And he laughed at me and said, 'You don't really believe that.' That was it. That was all he said, but it was how he said it. I wanted to cry but I laughed it off. Deep down, I thought, 'Yes, I do believe that. How dare you tell me what to think.' But what Cuthbert did was not so unusual. My father did it—"Don't worry your pretty head."—was what he said. My mother said, 'Stop being so melodramatic.' Isn't that what we're told all our lives, not to feel a thing, think nothing for ourselves, especially if you're a woman. I don't want to raise Henry like that. I'm glad you're not like that. I'm starting to think there was something to your philosophers. If I do read them, will you talk to me about them?"

"Read anything you like."

"There again. Cuthbert would never say such a thing."

Isabella got up to freshen up for dinner. Frederick sipped his wine and went back to his book, but he didn't see the pages. His life was good. He had no complaints. He and Isabella were friends. That was all they would ever be, but he had not the heart for anything else. In these moments, he would slip back into the melancholy and he would miss Ellie.

On the worst days, Frederick went for walks down by the docks as there wasn't a good beach to visit. They had to go up the coast a bit if they wanted any sea bathing, but the docks and smell of the salt air were enough for Frederick. He let himself conjure the moments of his time at the cabin and when he watched Abby playing in the sand. He'd long lost his last fragment of the salmon shell, but the scar where it cut him was still on his finger. He wondered why it wasn't enough to bind Ellie to him, but no, the shell was from Abby, not Ellie. He wondered how they got on and if he would ever see her again. Maybe someday. Isabella's new friends didn't care about divorce. They were all progressive enough, and they wouldn't abandon her. They liked her for who she was and not the connections or money she brought. He didn't particularly want a divorce. He loved little Henry as if he were his own, but there was something behind the veil he had with Ellie that lifted the melancholy, something that could be gotten from no one else.

TO MASTER THE TIDES

Frederick stayed out late that day and kept walking near the ocean well past the docks. The land was rocky, and the waves splashed up in between. Frederick stood on them, looking far out to sea. The sun shone where he was but there was a storm there. He imagined what it would be like to be on a ship in the midst of that. Not one of the newer ships that burned coal to power its engine but a man of war, like the pirates sailed. What did it feel like to be tossed by a wave taller than your ship? He imagined himself sinking down, down, down—the weight of the water crushing his chest. How deep was the ocean? Could he make it to where the storm was? But he wouldn't. He'd promised Ellie.

The water lapped up on the rocks. The tide was coming in a few hours. Frederick ought to go back or he would be late for supper. He watched the water's edge coming in and out; even here the ripples were getting stronger from the distant storm. Wedged in the rocks was a salmon-colored shell. This one was from a clam, not the same kind as the swirled one Abby gave him, but the same color. He picked it up and wiped off the sand and seaweed.

You knew what I was thinking, Ellie. I'm going to believe this shell is from you. My tides are at bay now. I hope that yours are, too.

The months went on. Frederick and Isabella watched Henry grow. Isabella was truly happy with her work and son. Frederick found it easier to pretend. He kept the new shell by his bed and traced its lines each night with the scarred fingertip. He wouldn't allow himself to consciously think of them, the Fae women he knew were out there somewhere. When he thought of them, it pressed on him too much.

JOSEPHINE BORGIA

Isabella caught him one of the few times his mind wandered. She seemed so worried. He passed it off as an upset stomach. But the shell. The shell tethered him to the Fae world still.

Maybe that was the problem. The Fae world. He wanted back behind the veil and there was no path there now. He wanted Ellie. If he was honest with himself, that's all he wanted, but he stood by Isabella. He raised her son and took some joy in that. Still, though the tides no longer troubled him, the melancholy would not lift. Isabella gave up asking him when he seemed troubled. He told her all at first, but he could sense her frustration when she could do nothing to help. She did care for him, even if it was only one flesh-and-blood human to another. He cared for her the same way and didn't want to trouble her anymore. Those thoughts crept back, but each night he would look at his shell and remember he promised Ellie.

A full year after they moved to Newcastle, they had a visitor from the old county. Frederick and Isabella had tea on the terrace that day. Fat little Henry waddled around in the garden while one of the maids chased him around the new Poseidon statue. The statue was frightfully ugly, but Frederick liked it all the same. Henry was eager to climb it, but his pudgy little hands couldn't yet reach the base.

"He's gotten big," came a voice from the doorway. Frederick and Isabella turned to see Kilkenny coming out to the garden. Behind him was Abby. She had grown much since Frederick last saw her. She was 7 now, closer to 8. She wore a broad-brimmed travel hat and her hair had darkened to a rich butter color, tied up with a blue bow. She held the hand of a small boy about Henry's age, but still struggling to keep his feet. Abby smiled up at Frederick. Frederick only stared as if he couldn't believe she was really there.

"What a charming little girl!" said Isabella when she saw the children. "She reminds me of that portrait of your mother, the one in the library at your father's townhouse."

"Yes, she does have the same color eyes," Frederick said.

Isabella went over to the children and steered them to the table on the patio. "What is your name? Is this your brother?"

"I'm Abby, and this is Edward."

Isabella picked up the little boy, who fell asleep on her shoulder as if he hadn't slept his whole life long. "What charming names. I have a little boy as well. Would you like some cake?" Isabella smiled at the men and waved them off. She knew Frederick would tell her all later. Frederick and Kilkenny went for a walk in the small garden.

"She seems to like children," said Kilkenny.

"She always wanted a large family, I think, but it wasn't in the cards for us."

"She may still have it, depending on you."

"What do you mean?"

"Is there a place for you to sit down, Estibus?"

Ellie was dead. The words resonated through Frederick's head like an ocean storm crushing a ship at sea. Frederick did sit, on the ground where he was and cried. He didn't care what Kilkenny thought of him. He cried like a child the second the words were spoken. Kilkenny sat on the ground next to him and waited until he got it all out. The solicitor clapped him on the back when it was all through.

"Want to go in and have a drink?"

JOSEPHINE BORGIA

Frederick nodded and followed his friend into the house, careful not to turn towards Isabella or the children when he passed by. Frederick sat by the fire while Kilkenny poured drinks. He handed him a brandy and sat across from him.

"We can go over everything tomorrow if you're not up to it."

"Go over everything?" Frederick was still in a daze.

"Yes, but there's a lot."

"Tell me what happened. What are the children to do?"

Stanway had gone first. His life of dissipation caught up to him, but he was sick on top of that. Consumption infected his lungs first, which he might have lived with for a few more years had not cancer joined it. In the end, there was fever and infection on top of it all. Ellie nursed him through until the end. In her fatigue, she caught something from her brother. As strong as she was, it got the better of her, too.

"She's left the children a good deal of money," said Kilkenny. "No one had any idea she had that much. Her father was a good businessman, but she made some investments, too. Smart enough to pull it all out before the panic in '93. She's left their money in trust with you as the executor."

Frederick was quiet. He waited for Kilkenny to ask how many of the old rumors were true, but the questions didn't come.

"Where are the children to go?" Frederick asked.

"That's up to you," said Kilkenny. "She asked me if you could help them find a place."

"You saw her?"

"Aye, at the end."

TO MASTER THE TIDES

"They can come here, of course. I'll adopt them. Isabella will be happy. Henry will have playmates."

Isabella did readily take the children in and the house became lively all at once. Edward, being so young, soon cheered at Isabella's attention and in the giggles of his new friend. The boy had Ellie's heart-shaped face all over again. Frederick and Isabella often sat on the terrace and watched the children play, Abby keeping the two boys in line as much as she could.

"Do you think he's yours, Frederick?" said Isabella one day. "There is a look here and there and then about his eyes. His hair is curling up, too, just like yours. He's about the right age, isn't he?"

Frederick said nothing and watched the little boy run in the grass.

"I hope he is," Isabella said. "I'm glad he's with his father."

Even after the children came, the melancholy continued for Frederick. He had a habit of sitting on the front porch in the evenings to have a smoke and a drink by himself. He allowed the melancholy to take over then, just until the sun finished setting. When it was down, he put it away for the day. One evening, Abby came out carrying a box and joined him. Normally, he liked to be alone, but she seemed sad as he was. She didn't talk of her mother's death much. He wished she would but was waiting until she was ready. Abby set the box on the table beside the chair and climbed into Frederick's lap. She laid her head on his shoulder and Frederick put an arm around her while she snuggled into his chest.

"Uncle and Mama were changelings, you know," she said.

"Your mother told me something like that once."

JOSEPHINE BORGIA

"Uncle had to go back to the Fae and Mama went with him to make sure they let him back in since he causes so much trouble. I couldn't go because I'm only half, and Edward, he's three-quarters, but they won't take him, either."

"Three quarters? Where did the other quarter come from?"

"From your mama, of course. My mama told me. The sea was always quiet for her, so she had to be a water Fae."

Frederick bit his lip. Edward was his boy, after all. He knew but it didn't hit him until Abby spoke the words.

"Mama said you could help me," Abby went on.

"Me? I'm not much help for anything, but I'll try for you. Why did she think I could help?"

"Because you knew what it was like."

"What?"

"To be half fairy and long for your true home, but never be able to go there. It makes you melancholy. But this world is beautiful, too. She said you would help me find it and it would help with the sadness."

"Are you sad, little one?" asked Frederick, squeezing her closer.

"Sometimes, when I miss mama."

"I miss her very much, too, but we'll remember her together, won't we?" Together they would remember Ellie. He would fight through the last tide of melancholy and they would best it together.

Frederick waited until later to open the box Abby gave to him. He couldn't blame the girl for waiting. It had been so hard for her to give away anything that had been her mother's. He opened it alone in his room. It was tied with a knotted string, but he wouldn't cut it. It took him a good twenty minutes to pick the knot apart. Inside was a full cigarette case stuffed full of fairy rolled cigarettes and a letter. The letter was short, and it wasn't signed but even in the weak lines, he recognized the swirling hand.

I'm going to ask you a selfish thing. I rolled you all the cigarettes I had strength to roll. I know how sentimental you are. I could tell from the beginning, but damn you, Frederick, smoke them. Smoke them and remember me and when you've done with them, be done with me. I loved you, and you loved me and that is more than any of us can hope for. I know you couldn't stay. You couldn't stay with me and be the man I loved. We were doomed from the start you and I, but such is the way with human and Fae.

Frederick tucked the letter in his breast pocket, took a cigarette out of the case, and lit it.

CPSIA information can be obtained
at www.ICGtesting.com
Printed in the USA
JSHW060741310822
29806JS00006B/55